The Principal's Kid

The Principal's Kid

A Lion and Bobbi Mystery

Joan Weir

POLESTAR

BOOK PUBLISHERS

Polestar Book Publishers acknowledges the ongoing support
of The Canada Council; the British Columbia Ministry of
Small Business, Tourism and Culture through the BC Arts
Council; and the Government of Canada through the Book
Publishing Development Program (BPIDP).

Cover art by Ljuba Levstek.
Cover design by Jim Brennan.
Printed and bound in Canada.

CANADIAN CATALOGUING IN PUBLICATION DATA
        Weir, Joan, 1928-
        The principal's kid
        ISBN 1-896095-98-4
        I. Title.
        PS8595.E48P74 1999   jC813'.54   C99-910215-X
        PZ7.W438Pr 1999

LIBRARY OF CONGRESS CATALOGUE NUMBER: 99-61832

POLESTAR BOOK PUBLISHERS
P.O. Box 5238, Station B
Victoria, British Columbia
Canada   V8R 6N4
http://mypage.direct.ca/p/polestar/

In the United States:
P.O. Box 468
Custer, WA
USA   98240-0468

5 4 3 2 1

Canada

With thanks to Phoebe Kingscote of Tanglewood Farm and to the staff at the Powell River Tourist Bureau for your interest and input.

Chapter 1

The message light on the answering machine was blinking when Lion arrived in the kitchen. Rubbing the sleep out of his eyes he glanced at the clock over the sink. No wonder he hadn't heard the phone. It was still only half past nine. Nobody was up at half past nine during the summer holidays.

For a minute he wondered why his sister hadn't heard the phone ringing and answered it, for she was usually up earlier than he was. Besides, most of the calls were for her. Then he remembered. Bobbi had said last night she was going to take Brie out for an early morning ride before it got too hot.

He pressed the "play" button on the answering machine.

The call wasn't for his sister but for his dad. "Syd, it's Jock," said a voice Lion recognized, a longtime friend of Dad's. But instead of the casual leisured tone Lion expected, Jock sounded curt and hurried. "Since it's only seven-thirty, I was hoping you wouldn't have left yet for that law office of yours, but I'd forgotten what an early bird you are." Disappointment was clearly evident in Jock's voice. The words began coming even more quickly. "I'm at my fishing place in Powell River and I need to talk to you about something fairly important. I've already sent a note to your office, but I didn't want to include any specific details in case other people might read it. I'll try to phone again later if my line is clear. Otherwise, will you phone me as soon as you get home? Sorry for the rush, but I'm afraid this can't wait."

The machine clicked off.

Lion pushed the "save" button so the message would be there for Dad when he came home at suppertime, and turned his attention to breakfast.

Chapter 2

Dad joined Lion and Bobbi at the dinner table that evening in frowning silence.

He'd been relaxed and joking when he'd first arrived home. Even after he'd listened to that strange telephone message he'd still been only mildly puzzled. It wasn't till he'd phoned his friend Jock three times at ten minute intervals and had still received no answer that the worried frown had come into his eyes.

Now he sat in withdrawn silence, not even glancing at the fried chicken on the plate in front of him, alternating between rereading a letter in his hand and staring thoughtfully into space.

That must be the note Jock had referred to in his phone message, Lion decided. He glanced inquiringly across the table at his sister.

From Bobbi's answering nod it was clear she was thinking the same thing.

Unable to contain his curiosity any longer, Lion said casually, "What's so puzzling?"

For a minute Dad gave no sign that he'd heard, then Lion's question penetrated. "I'm not sure," he said slowly. "I'd say the whole thing was a joke if it involved anyone but Jock. But he's not the sort of man to deal in foolish jokes." He continued to stare at the letter.

Pushing at the shock of blond hair that, as usual, was falling forward over his forehead, Lion glanced a second time at his sister. She was fourteen, two years older than he was, and particularly since Mom had left, Dad sometimes told her things about his law cases that he didn't mention to Lion. But the brief shake of Bobbi's head made it clear that this time she was as much in the dark as he was.

Well, if he couldn't find out what was going on, he might as well take advantage of Dad's preoccupation, he decided, and without bothering to ask permission helped himself to another large piece of chicken.

Dad's preoccupation wasn't as deep as Lion had thought. "I hope you intend to eat more than just chicken," Dad said dryly, nodding at Lion's plate. "For instance that untouched helping of vegetables."

"But it's broccoli and brussels sprouts!"

"Broccoli and brussels sprouts are good for you."

He couldn't eat them — he'd be sick! But Dad looked as if he was moving into his Neanderthal stage. He had to think of something …

Inspiration struck. "Have you ever thought about how much harm can result from making kids eat things that are good for them?" he said brightly.

Dad's eyebrows lifted.

"It's true," Lion rushed on before Dad could interrupt. "It can absolutely destroy a guy's self-confidence. Think about it. If a kid is constantly being told to eat things because they're good for him, it means only one thing — that he needs help. If he was already an okay human being he wouldn't need brussel sprouts or broccoli! How many guys who are convinced they aren't okay human beings are gonna end up rocket scientists?"

"Somehow I've never pictured you as a rocket scientist," Dad returned dryly, "so at least for the time being I think it's safe for you to risk the broccoli and brussel sprouts."

Lion retreated in disarray. If he worked on it, maybe he could come up with a better argument.

In the meantime, Bobbi was staring at the letter still in Dad's hand. "Is something wrong?" she asked, tackling the question directly.

The amusement faded from Dad's face. "I honestly don't know." He glanced again at the open sheet in front of him. "You know Jock McPherson and I have been friends for years. For the past little while he has been heading up some kind of scientific study for the Fisheries Department in Victoria. That's where he's living now. But he loves to fish so he also keeps a place at Powell River. Whenever he has a few days off he heads up there and he and his fishing partner Devon spend their time catching prawns." Dad continued to stare at the handwritten page, his face creased in a frown. "Funny. In all the years we've been friends he's never before written me a letter. Whenever we want to get in touch, we phone. It doesn't make sense that he would suddenly decide to write, follow up the letter with a phone message urging me to phone back, then not bother to be in to receive my call."

Lion hadn't watched years of TV detective shows for nothing. "It makes perfect sense if somebody is bugging his phone," he retorted. "And obviously somebody is, or Jock wouldn't have included that bit about phoning you back again later if his line was clear."

For the first time since sitting down at the table Dad relaxed and smiled. "I'm ashamed to admit that thought occurred to me as well — but only briefly."

"That's the reason he phoned so early this morning," Lion rushed on, encouraged by Dad's unexpected agreement. His voice rose as he warmed to his theory. "And that's why he sounded disappointed when you weren't here, because he'd been counting on that being the one time he could phone without anyone listening."

11

"If he knew his phone was being bugged he'd never have asked Dad to phone him back," Bobbi said in disgust.

"He would if he figured there was another time right around dinner when the listeners wouldn't be on duty," Lion returned, addressing Bobbi but watching Dad. "He was probably right there by the phone when Dad called, but didn't dare pick up the receiver because he knew the listener was back on duty."

Instead of disagreeing, Dad looked thoughtful.

"See! Dad agrees!" Lion told his sister, trying not to gloat. It wasn't often that Dad went along with one of his theories — particularly if it had anything to do with spies or espionage.

"Well, I don't agree," Bobbi retorted, "and I don't believe Dad does either." She turned to her father. "Explain to young Sherlock that just because someone writes you a letter, then gets detained and isn't in when you phone back, it isn't exactly convincing proof that the person is in trouble."

"True," Dad agreed. "But before we argue any more, perhaps I should read you what Jock says in his letter." He picked up the single sheet. "Greetings, Syd," he read. "How about getting out of that dull law office for a few days and coming fishing with me. You'd be surprised how interesting the view can be from my window. As you know, prawns are a valuable resource up here, and as a result prawn theft is big business — nothing new about that. But in places where the prawn have octopus for neighbours there seems to be a new wrinkle.

"Speaking of octopus, you probably don't like them, and I don't like them either. But if sometime you can't avoid them, don't worry. They're playful and friendly. You'll find they really aren't scary even with all those arms. It's only when they're divided by four that they get vicious.

"Please come if you can, and soon. From all the signs, I've an idea the calm weather won't hold much longer. I'm counting on you. Jock."

"That's not a letter asking for help," Bobbi said in disgust. "It's a joke."

"You think it's a joke because you don't watch the right TV shows," Lion told her, his eyes gleaming excitedly. He turned to Dad. "Not only is it a call for help, it's an urgent call for help. That's what the last bit means — the part about the calm weather not holding much longer. Spies on TV always talk like that in their code messages. I agree with Bobbi that the octopus stuff is probably nonsense, and maybe the bit about the view, but that's to put people off, in case someone's opening his mail as well as tapping his phone line."

Dad's eyebrows lifted in surprise. "I had no idea you were such an authority on spy tactics. I'm impressed." His voice was dry. "Remind me to limit your TV viewing to one hour a day and only during pre-school programming."

Instead of being offended, Lion grinned. "That just proves how long it's been since you watched any kids' cartoons. It's a wonder anybody under the age of eight ever sleeps without nightmares." He took another huge mouthful of chicken and said around it, "So, are you gonna check that letter out?"

Dad's face sobered. "I think I have to. Jock really might be asking for help. Besides, there's a — " He broke off and all at once it seemed his attention was needed on selecting a roll from the tray. He began breaking it into pieces. "As I think I mentioned not long ago, I sort of half promised to make a trip up to Powell River anyway." He continued to concentrate on his roll. "An old friend of mine who lives there now is worried about her son. She'd like me to try to straighten out a mess he seems to have gotten himself into connected with the summer job he's been doing. If we go up to check on Jock, I can have a look at the job tangle as well."

The self-conscious note in Dad's voice had been making Lion more and more uncomfortable, but the unexpected use of "we" pushed that into the background. "You mean Bobbi and I can come too?"

"If you'd like to. After all, it's still summer holidays."

"Excellent!" Trusting that Dad had forgotten about the brussel sprouts and broccoli, Lion stuffed the last large mouthful of chicken into his mouth and continued thickly, "Maybe this will turn out to be another neat case like that last one. Then Bobbi and I will be able to help you track down the bad — "

"Then Bobbi and you can stay right out of it," Dad interrupted dryly, spacing the words apart for emphasis. "Last time both you and your sister conveniently suffered memory loss about staying out of danger and leaving the investigation of my case to me. This time I want your word that you will *not* interfere. And don't talk with your mouth full."

Lion swallowed the mouthful of chicken half chewed. "But you needed us! If we hadn't been there to help investigate, Spud might have died down that deserted mine shaft!"

"So might you, in case you've forgotten."

Lion's mouth went dry. It was true. He'd come closer than he ever wanted to come again to being buried alive down a mine shaft.

But there was no way anyone could get into any danger in Powell River. Dad might need him and Bobbi. And if he did, they couldn't refuse to help.

Chapter 3

"Of course, we'll take the horses," Dad announced, getting to his feet and preparing to leave the dining room.

Lion stared in disbelief. What was this "of course" bit? If Jock's letter was hinting at prawn theft some 350 feet below the surface of the ocean, exactly how did Dad think two dumb horses could help in the investigation? He asked the question aloud in a voice that held more than a trace of generation gap.

Dad's eyebrows lifted marginally. "It doesn't matter if Jock's letter is hinting at prawn theft, grand larceny or murder on the high seas, you and your sister are taking no part in it. Is that clear? I'm the one going up there to find out if something is wrong. You and your sister are going sightseeing, and for sightseeing you'll need either bicycles or horses." A smile pulled briefly at the corners of his mouth. "Considering the hilliness of the countryside, and your tolerance level for hard exercise, I suggest you settle on horses and let them do the climbing for you."

For a moment even Bobbi looked confused. "But isn't Powell River right on the coast?"

"Yes, but directly behind the town and extending both north and south are farming areas, dense forests, a thriving logging industry, and wonderful hiking and riding trails. In fact," Dad told her with a smile, "people travel to Powell River from all over the continent for the hiking and canoeing."

Bobbi seemed delighted at this Chamber of Commerce promotion, but Lion felt a sinking feeling somewhere deep inside. The two things he hated most in the whole world were sightseeing and horses.

No, that wasn't exactly true. Sightseeing and horses were the things he hated second most. What he hated most was having the teachers on his back calling him a slacker if he didn't top the Honour Roll, since his dad was a famous criminal lawyer, and then having all the kids on his back calling him a teachers' pet if he did. Talk about an image problem. Every time the guys passed around an answer on a test, or paid one of the school brains to do their homework, he could feel them wondering if he was going to blow the whistle.

It didn't help the night Tony and Brad decided to raid one of the teacher's gardens. He'd stayed back on the sidewalk and watched because he didn't want to be involved. But when the lights suddenly came on and Mr. Matioli came rushing out yelling, Tony and Brad accused him of deliberately standing on the sidewalk to draw attention to what was going on so they'd get in trouble.

It was the same the night the guys decided to spray paint some neat slogans on the outside wall of the school. He didn't take part because he figured it was a pointless thing to do. Instead he took off and headed home. A little while later the cops turned up. Though neither Tony nor Brad actually said so right out, he knew they figured he'd told on them to his dad, and because Dad was a big lawyer he must have called the police.

For a while after that Tony was kind of distant, which hurt because Tony was one of his best friends. So sometimes now he went along with things he didn't really want to do just to prove he was no different from the rest of the guys.

Under half-lowered lids he studied his sister across the table. Girls must be different, he decided, because

Dad's job didn't seem to raise an image problem for Bobbi. If she didn't want to do something she just opted out with no problem. Like this sightseeing business. It sounded sissy if a guy spent all his time sightseeing, but Bobbi could do it every day of the week if she —

With a start he realized that his sister was watching. Had what he'd been thinking shown on his face? Quickly he gave her a sunny smile. It wasn't that he didn't want to do things with her. They'd had a great time on that trip to Wells. He just wished the things they were going to do this time could be scuba diving and catching international prawn thieves. The guys would be impressed with that. But sightseeing with the horses?

"Whichever you decide on, bicycles or horses," Dad's words broke into Lion's preoccupation, "be ready for an early start in the morning. We've a long way to go and two ferries to time." He got to his feet. "And eat your vegetables. We've already agreed they're good for you."

At the amused note in Dad's voice Lion looked up quickly, but Dad was already at the door.

Resigned, Lion turned his attention to the vegetables. "Yuck!" he muttered feelingly. Stuffing his mouth full, he washed the green mess down with a huge glass of milk, then picking up his plate headed for the kitchen. "I'll help load the dishwasher as soon as I get something to take away the taste," he told Bobbi, who was rinsing the plates and putting them into the machine. Reaching for a box of chocolate cookies, he stuffed two into his mouth. Then realizing his sister was paying no attention, he added a third. Then for the first time it occurred to him that Bobbi wasn't just off in some private thought world — she seemed upset. Was it something he'd done? But if so, why wasn't she glaring at him? Instead she seemed hardly aware that he was in the room.

"What is it? What's up?" he asked, moving closer. Picking up the last two dirty plates he rinsed them under the hot water then added them to the dishwasher. For a moment Bobbi continued working in silence, then she turned a tense face toward him. "I know it sounds dumb, but I'm scared."

"Scared of what?"

"I'm not sure. But I've got this feeling — " She left the rest hanging.

A familiar nag of uneasiness started up in Lion's middle, for his sister's "feelings" had an uncanny way of proving true. It had been her "feeling" that the witcher in Dad's last case might be in danger that had got them shot at, smothered unconscious, and almost sealed alive down a deserted mine shaft. He wasn't about to admit it, but all three of those activities placed fairly low on his wish list of things to do again.

"Someone is going to be in danger," Bobbi went on in a low voice. "I can feel it. That's why I'm scared."

"Someone like who?"

"Dad maybe — or Jock — or maybe the lady Dad is going to visit."

Lion wanted to say that it was okay with him so long as it was that lady who was in danger, for he hadn't forgotten that funny note that had crept into Dad's voice when he'd talked about her. But he had an idea Bobbi might not think this was the time to joke.

Besides, Bobbi had really meant it about being scared. She wouldn't pretend to be scared if she wasn't — not mega scared. Not when her success rate at danger forecasting was almost one hundred percent. A person didn't mess around with a reputation like that. In which case this trip might turn out to be okay after all. International prawn thieves and everybody in danger. He and Bobbi might have to save ...

"But Dad could be right about taking the horses instead of bikes," Bobbi continued. A subtle change had come into her voice. The worry had gone. Now she sounded innocent. Closing the dishwasher she turned it on, then started toward the kitchen door. "Bikes would be okay if we were just going sightseeing, but I guess we could need the horses for chasing international prawn thieves."

"Funny! Funny!" Lion returned, struggling to recover. He should have known his sister would guess what he was thinking and razz him about it. "But if Dad's right about it being too hilly for bikes, then okay, we'll take the horses. Only that one of mine had better not try any more dump the rider games."

Bobbi was already starting across the yard. She glanced back without breaking stride. "Tell him."

"No way! If I say anything it'll put the idea in his head, then for sure he'll dump me."

"Don't be dumb."

Lion didn't bother to answer.

A few minutes later they'd reached the tack shed at the top end of the pasture. Bobbi moved inside. Picking up two halters, she handed one to Lion. Then she filled the bottom of a bucket with oats and continued down the pasture toward where Rajah and Brie were grazing.

Reluctantly, Lion followed.

They lived on two acres of green pasture land just twenty kilometres out of the city in the centre of a sleepy suburb. Their sprawling ranch-style house sat next to the road. Behind it, ringed by clumps of tall pines and spruce trees, was a large fenced pasture containing a corral and a three-sided wooden shelter that the horses could use when they wanted to escape the cold or the rain or the wind. But most of the time they preferred to stay out and graze in the pasture, as they were doing now. Brie was at the far end next to the bottom fence. Raj was about halfway along.

At their approach Brie kept grazing but Rajah's head came up. Seeing Bobbi, he whinnied and started toward her.

"See?" Bobbi said continuing to walk toward the horses. "He's glad to see you."

"He's glad to see you," Lion corrected. "Obviously his night vision isn't too good. He hasn't noticed yet that I'm here too."

"It's not night yet and his vision's perfect," Bobbi began, but at that moment Raj noticed Lion. He stopped moving.

"Dumb horse," Lion said disgustedly. "Can't you see the wheels turning in his thick skull? Now watch. He's gonna turn and walk away."

"Not if you call him."

Lion remained silent and Raj continued to stare.

"Come on, Lion. Call him. That's what he's waiting for. He wants to know you're going to be friendly. Tell him hello. I bet anything he'll start coming toward us again."

"I'm not telling any horse hello."

"Don't be so stubborn. Then don't say hello, but call him."

"And give him a chance to make me look like a fool?"

"He won't make you look like a fool. He's waiting for you to make the first move."

For another moment Lion resisted, then trying not to sound as stupid as he felt, he managed, "Raj!"

The big gelding continued to stand motionless, watching.

"Call him again."

"Come on, Raj! Come on, you big lunk."

20

Raj's tail swished high over his back, then as if he'd been intending to do it all the time, he started moving leisurely forward.

"Hey, how about that," Lion began, grinning. But the grin was short lived, for Raj wasn't moving in a straight line. He was moving in a wide leisurely circle — back the way he'd come.

Bobbi dissolved in laughter.

"Confounded horse!" Lion called after him. "If you're not careful I'll tell Dad I've decided not to keep you after all!"

Raj gave no sign of hearing but continued his leisurely saunter in the opposite direction.

"Now will you agree that he hates me?" Lion kicked a pebble in the direction of the departing Raj. "And stop laughing."

"I can't help it. But he doesn't hate you. If he did he'd ignore you. He's playing games." She held out the oats bucket. "Here. Take him these and offer a truce."

"Never."

Bobbi sighed. "Give me your halter." She put it over her shoulder, together with the other one. "The trouble is you're two of a kind — each as stubborn and pig-headed as the other."

"It would serve him right if I didn't ride him after all!" Lion retorted.

"But then how would you catch those international prawn thieves?" Bobbi asked innocently.

She didn't wait for an answer, but moved through the shadows to the bottom of the pasture to give Brie and Rajah a final treat before bed.

Chapter 4

"So, tell us more about Jock," Lion said, resting his arms along the back of the front seat of the station wagon so his head was almost level with Bobbi's.

Dad's eyes met his in the driver's rearview mirror. "Have you forgotten our agreement? If you come with me you stay right out of things."

"Who said anything about getting involved? But talking about it could help." A new idea struck and Lion's voice brightened. "That's what Mulder and Scully always do when they're on a case. They bounce ideas back and forth with each other and that helps them work out what's —" He broke off abruptly at the expression on Dad's face. Obviously the *X-Files* wasn't one of Dad's favourite TV shows. But that was no reason to give up. "I know it hasn't occurred to you," he substituted brightly, "but you really might need us."

Again Dad's glance met Lion's briefly in the rearview mirror. His eyebrows lifted. "You're right," he admitted thoughtfully. "That idea hadn't occurred to me. But now that it has, I promise to banish it immediately. Do up your seat belt."

"It is."

"Then tighten it."

Resigned, Lion sat back in his seat and fastened the belt properly.

For the past few minutes Bobbi had been growing increasingly uneasy. "Will you promise something, Dad?" she said at last, turning sideways in the passenger seat toward him. "Will you promise to be careful and not take any risks?"

Taking one hand briefly off the wheel, Dad covered Bobbi's hand with his and smiled down at her. "Of course I won't take any risks. I never do. You know that."

"I know it sounds dumb," Bobbi went on, fidgeting with the buckle on her seat belt as it lay across her lap, "but ever since last night I've had this feeling that something dangerous is going to happen."

Again Dad squeezed her hand. "Stop worrying, honey. I know there have been several times in the past when those feelings of yours turned out to be right, but it was always associated with some case I was working on. I'm not on a case this time. I'm just going as a friend to see if I can help Mrs. Hamilton straighten out the tangle her son seems to have got into, and make sure Jock isn't in trouble."

"You said he was heading up some kind of study for the Fisheries Department," Bobbi went on. "What sort of study?"

"Something to do with the effects of dioxin and furan on marine life. Actually, Mrs. Hamilton is the person who pushed the Fisheries people into sponsoring this study."

"What are dioxin and furan?"

"Two of the elements in the effluent from pulp mills. Sometimes they get too high."

Bobbi frowned. "There can't be anything very dangerous about that."

"Of course not," Dad agreed. "This study Jock is doing is purely a research thing. As for his concerns about the prawn fishing, he and his partner Devon fish purely as a hobby. If someone is helping himself to some of their catch, as Jock's letter seems to be suggesting, Jock will certainly speak up and protest, but he won't carry it to the point where anyone would be in any danger."

"Maybe the danger is from that deep water," Bobbi

suggested. "You said prawn traps were set 350 or 400 feet below the surface."

"So they are. But they aren't filled or dumped 350 feet below the surface. They're pulled up onto the deck of a boat to be emptied and rebaited."

Bobbi didn't say any more, but Lion could tell from the tight look of her shoulders that she wasn't convinced. Still, right now he had something more important to think about.

Was the real reason Dad was going all the way to Powell River to help Jock, or was it to help that lady, Mrs. Hamilton? He'd said her son was in some kind of trouble connected with his summer job. That probably meant shoplifting. Since when did Vancouver's busiest and most successful criminal lawyer spend his time travelling around the country defending some young kid caught shoplifting?

Lion said so aloud.

"It isn't shoplifting, he hasn't been caught, and I'm not defending him," Dad retorted. "At least I'm not defending him officially. All I'm hoping to do is present a brief to the court on behalf of all the boys and ask for leniency."

Lion's interest was finally caught. "You mean it's not just this one kid? There are several of them?" Dad nodded.

"What did they do?" Dad paused to negotiate a curve on the highway, then he continued, "It all seems to centre around a pretty ingenious housebreaking scam."

Lion's spirits lifted markedly. "Ingenious clever?"

"Ingenious very clever. And very original."

Loosening his seatbelt slightly, Lion leaned closer. "How did it work?"

For a moment Dad didn't answer. He was watching a red van that had moved up behind them. Lion had noticed it too. It seemed to be behind them most the way. It kept moving up as if to pass, then changing its mind and dropping back again. A really chicken-hearted driver, Lion decided. He had to be if he was afraid to pass the horsetrailer. What did he think was going to happen? That the horses were going to kick out at him? Well, if he was that chicken he'd just have to stay behind, because Dad never drove quickly when they were pulling the horses.

Dad continued to watch the van in his sideview mirror. Again, as it had done several times before, after moving right up behind as if to pass, the van had slowed and again dropped back.

Dad returned his attention to the conversation. "As for how it worked, that's one of the things I'm intending to find out. So far all the boys seem to be telling a different story. Nobody seems clear on what the real point behind it was, or who was primarily responsible."

"But you suspect the son of this lady?"

"No. I don't think C.J. even realized what was going on. Not till afterward. However his mother is afraid someone deliberately set him up to take the blame."

"He calls himself C.J.?" Lion put in. "Talk about dumb."

"Almost as dumb as calling yourself Lion instead of Lionel," Bobbi suggested sweetly.

"You wouldn't say that if your name was Lionel."

"Did it occur to you that he might not like his name, either?"

"He's still got to be dumb. He should have caught on that something was going on and got the heck out of there. Then nobody could have set him up for anything."

"What if by the time he realized it, he was already set-up as fall-guy?" Dad put in quietly.

To that Lion didn't have an answer.

"Also, there's another complication," Dad went on. "The men his mother thinks have set him up are also his employers."

"Pardon?"

"Since the summer holidays started, C.J. has been working down at the wharf in Powell River, unloading and rebaiting prawn traps. Virginia suspects that the men who are hiring him to tend the prawn traps may be the ones behind the housebreaking scam."

At the unexpected use of Mrs. Hamilton's first name Lion felt a sudden stab of worry, but he pushed it away. Concentrating instead on the main issue, he said, "You mean he's still working for them? Even when he suspects they've set him up for something? Any sixteen year old who can't see — "

"He's not sixteen."

"Dad, he's got to be." Lion used the forbearing tone he always used when the generation gap was showing. "If he wasn't sixteen he couldn't get a job."

"I'm glad you pointed that out, son. I wonder, then, if his mother could be mistaken. She thinks those men were able to hire him when he was underage because it's a part-time job and a private arrangement just between themselves, but perhaps that's not true. Perhaps C.J. has been fooling her all these years. Perhaps he's really much older than she realizes —"

Bobbi burst out laughing.

"So, okay, how old is he?" Lion said struggling to recover.

"Fourteen. The same as Bobbi."

For a minute Lion turned his attention to the scenery outside the car window while he adjusted to having lost that round. "So, fourteen is old enough to know that if the

26

guys you're working for are setting you up for something it's time to quit," he said at last. "Why didn't he? Or why didn't his mom make him?"

"I'll answer those two questions separately," Dad replied. "C.J. doesn't want to quit because he's convinced the only way to clear himself is to hang around until he finds out what's going on. And his mother doesn't want to make him quit because she's afraid everybody else will read *fired* in place of *quit*, and see his leaving as proof that he really is guilty of something."

"Why aren't the police doing anything?" Bobbi asked in a puzzled tone.

"Because they're not sure yet that the whole thing might not be a boyish prank. They suspect something much bigger is behind it, but so far they can't seem to get their hands on any solid evidence. Houses were broken into in broad daylight, but they've no idea how because there is no trace of any damage to doors, or locks, or windows. Also, in more than half the cases nothing inside the houses was damaged or stolen. The only proof that someone had been there was that the TV was on and a polite thank-you note was left sitting on the coffee table."

"Hey! Neat! Sort of like Zorro!" Lion put in.

Dad glared at him in the rearview mirror.

"If nothing was stolen why is anybody concerned?" Bobbi asked.

"Because people don't like the thought of some stranger coming into their house during the day while they're at work, and perhaps snooping into their private business papers. Also, it wasn't true in every case that nothing was taken. In about half the break-ins a great many small valuables disappeared."

"That's evidence!" Bobbi said quickly. "Can't the police use that?"

Lion was still watching Dad in the rearview mirror. At Bobbi's words the corners of Dad's mouth pulled upward. "That's another strange twist. All the things that have disappeared seem to have disappeared into thin air. There is no trace of them being sold in local pawn shops, or being taken across the border. The police can't lay formal charges until they have something concrete to base them on."

"No corpus delicti!" Lion said delightedly. "Isn't that what they call it on TV when the murderer can't be convicted because the body has disappeared!"

Dad's eyebrows lifted marginally. "More or less. Yes. But before you decide to murder somebody I should warn you that getting rid of a body is not as easy as it sounds."

"Too bad," Bobbi said with feigned regret. "Otherwise, Dad, you and I could really simplify things around our house if we just got rid of — " She nodded significantly toward the back seat.

Lion laughed, then turned his attention to Dad. "So first we check on Jock, then we discover what's behind this house scam. Right?"

"Wrong." Dad moved the car into the inside lane to be ready for the Ferry Exit which was coming along in less than a kilometre. "First I will check on Jock, then I will act for C.J. and try to clear him of any wrongdoing. As for you and Bobbi, starting right this minute you two will concentrate on sightseeing."

Lion couldn't believe Dad could be so unadventurous! The only fun would be in working out what this weird scam was all about! Then another thought struck which pushed that one away. Dad seemed awfully concerned about some kid he'd never even met. "Is this guy's mom a good friend of yours?" he asked carefully.

"As a matter of fact she is." Again Dad glanced back in the rearview mirror. "An old school friend. She's principal of one of the big Middle Schools in Powell River. You'll like her. She's bright, intelligent, lots of fun, and really concerned about important things like the environment and wildlife habitat."

Lion's built-in trouble sensors snapped to attention. Why would Dad suddenly sound so enthusiastic? One glance at his sister in the seat ahead told him that Bobbi had caught the new note in Dad's voice, too. "How good an old school friend?" Lion managed.

This time as Dad glanced back in the rearview mirror his eyes were dancing. "What's that supposed to mean?"

"Nothing!" Lion tried to sound innocent. "I was just wondering if she was a — you know — a regular friend, or — or — sort of special?"

Dad's grin widened. "Are you asking whether or not I'm in love with her?"

"No way!" Lion struggled for words. " It's just — I — I mean — " He swallowed, then blurted impulsively, "Are you?"

"Not at the moment."

Lion started to breathe again.

"But who knows what might happen in the future."

"Dad! You can't be serious!"

"Why not?"

"Because —" Lion floundered. He couldn't tell his dad that it was way to soon for him to think of dating anybody new, or that Mom might still come back, or even that the last thing he and Bobbi needed was a school Principal for a stepmother, so he compromised. "Because you're thirty-seven!"

Dad's eyebrows lifted in surprise. "I'd quite forgotten that." His voice turned dry. "What a good thing you reminded me."

"Come on, Dad," Lion stammered. "You know what

I mean." He wished now that he hadn't been so piggish at breakfast. At the time he'd thought he might be in danger of dying of starvation before he had a chance to eat again so he'd demolished two huge bowls of cereal, a granola bar, four cookies and an apple. Now they congealed into a hard lump in his stomach. If Dad did have a crush on this woman —

"It seems I should restrict your viewing of TV soap operas as well as TV spy stories," Dad remarked dryly, still watching Lion's stricken expression in the rearview mirror.

It wasn't only his sister who could guess what he was thinking from his expression, Lion realized. That guy in the story who'd had to wear an iron mask was luckier than he'd thought!

"Before you have me love-stricken and married," Dad was continuing, "let me reassure you. We are only going to Powell River for a few days, and a few days isn't enough time to fall in love with anyone. We're just staying long enough to make sure Jock isn't in trouble and to help Virginia with her son."

Lion didn't argue, but two or three days was plenty of time to fall in love. Particularly when a person was already calling the other person by her first name! It happened on TV all the time.

Again Dad guessed what he was thinking. "You know, it might be a good thing if I did fall in love with this woman," he said casually. "We could all move to Powell River. I could run my law practice from there and you could enroll in Mrs. Hamilton's Middle School."

Bobbi laughed.

Lion didn't think it was the slightest bit funny. No guy could possibly survive in a school where his stepmother was Principal!

Chapter 5

The ferry officials noticed the horse trailer as soon as Dad drove up to the Horseshoe Bay Ferry Terminal. Immediately one of them moved forward and directed Dad to the far loading lane rather than having them stay in line with the rest of the traffic. Then when they reached the outside lane another official ushered them straight to the front.

"Hopefully, the horses will get as little carbon dioxide as possible," Dad explained. He pointed to one of several printed notices along the ferry wall asking motorists to turn off their car motors immediately after parking on the lower deck, and not to start up again until the ferry had reached the dock at the other end. "Unfortunately, people often ignore those notices. For any animals that have to stay down here for the whole trip the build up of CO_2 can be a problem."

"Maybe no cars will park right behind the trailer," Bobbi suggested, but within moments the cars and vans were bumper to bumper across the whole parking deck.

Bobbi started toward the rear door of the trailer to check the horses.

"Stick this in the trailer, too, will you?" Dad said, handing Bobbi his briefcase. "It's just in the way in the car."

"D'you want me to hide it somewhere?"

"No need. There's nothing important in it. Just some dull facts and figures that anyone can read who wants to."

Bobbi nodded. She put the briefcase in with the tack then turned to check the horses. Having made sure they were travelling comfortably, she closed and locked the trailer door, then followed Dad and Lion up on deck.

For the first few minutes the trip was interesting, then the slow pace grew monotonous. "Talk about boring," Lion complained.

Bobbi's eyes met Dad's over Lion's head. "As they say," she said, "there are two kinds of people — those who see the glass as half full, and those who see the glass as half empty."

Lion stopped frowning. He sat straighter. "You know, you're right," he said thoughtfully.

Even Dad looked pleased.

"And it doesn't really matter either way," Lion went on in the same cheery tone, "as long as there's an un-opened case of coke in the fridge."

Bobbi gave Lion a pained look.

He went back to scowling.

At last the ferry terminal at Langdale became visible on the skyline. "D'you want to go down to the lower deck and make sure the horses are okay?" Lion suggested.

Bobbi didn't need any urging. The loudspeaker announcement hadn't yet been made telling the passengers to return to their cars, but she was as bored as Lion with staring at the view.

As they came out onto the lower deck she moved directly toward the small door on the side of the trailer, so they could go through it rather than lowering the rear loading ramp. But as she reached it she stopped in surprise, for it was not quite closed. "I know I made sure this was shut before we left," she told Lion in a puzzled tone. "How could it —" Breaking off, she exclaimed in alarm, "The lock has been forced!"

Before either Bobbi or Lion could move, the small side door was thrust open from inside. A tall muscular man in a faded jean jacket jumped down, pushed past them roughly and strode away.

"Stop! What were you doing?" Bobbi called after him. The jean jacketed figure broke into a run.

Lion started after him, but the man was too fast. Dodging back and forth between the closely packed cars he ran the full length of the ferry, then disappeared up the stairs at the far end. By the time Lion reached the foot of the staircase the man had disappeared.

"Did you see him clearly enough to recognize him again?" Bobbi asked as Lion returned.

"Probably not. I didn't see his face, but he was taller than average and well muscled, if that helps." He grinned. "Like ten million other people he was wearing a jean jacket." He glanced into the trailer. "Are the horses okay?"

"They aren't even upset." Bobbi gazed around. "It doesn't make sense. Why would he have broken in here —" For the first time she noticed Dad's briefcase. It wasn't where she'd left it with the tack. It was pulled out in full sight, and it was open. "He must have thought there was something important in it, but Dad said there wasn't."

"He probably doesn't realize that even yet," Lion put in delightedly, "because we surprised him while he was still looking. Now he'll probably spend the rest of the day wondering what he might have missed."

Bobbi laughed. "Serves him right." Her face sobered. "Should we tell Dad?"

"We'll have to because that lock will have to be fixed. Also, it's his briefcase. But it seems too bad to have to worry Dad when we scared that guy away before he could take anything," Lion said.

What if looking through Dad's case wasn't the man's only reason for coming? What if he had come to do something else first — something more important?

The thought came out of nowhere, and Lion felt a shiver of uneasiness. He told Bobbi what he was thinking.

"If he did have something more important to do first, that would explain why he hadn't finished long ago. After all, checking out Dad's briefcase wouldn't have taken more than two minutes and we were up on deck for forty."

"Something more important to do like what?" Bobbi asked carefully.

"Maybe something that would keep Dad from getting to Powell River."

"If that's your idea of a joke — "

"I'm not joking, Bobbi!" Before she could say anything more he hurried on, "Remember we decided Jock suspected his phone was being tapped but risked a quick call in the early morning figuring the phone listeners might not be on duty that early. What if they were on duty? What if they heard Jock say he'd sent Dad a letter?"

"You mean they'd assume the letter had spelled out exactly what was going on, not just given vague hints?"

"They couldn't gamble that it hadn't," Lion agreed. "They probably figured that was the reason Dad was going to Powell River — that he might even have Jock's letter with him in his briefcase — and that the best thing for them to do was to change his mind about going. After all, if something really is going on, the last person they want sticking his nose in is a hot-shot criminal lawyer."

Bobbi's thoughts were still on Lion's previous comment. "Change Dad's mind about going to Powell River how?"

"If I was in their shoes," Lion said watching his sister carefully, "and if I wanted to stop us from going to Powell River, I'd probably do something either to the station wagon, or to the horses."

The colour drained from Bobbi's cheeks.

"The horses are your department," Lion continued in the same business-like voice. "Make sure they're okay —

check their food and water and stuff. I'll check the station wagon."

He started with the trailer hitch to make sure it was properly fastened, then he checked the tires on both the car and the trailer. Next he made a complete circle around both the car and the trailer, looking underneath.

Everything seemed normal.

One final check, he decided, and walked all the way around again, only this time instead of looking underneath he peered through the slightly open car windows at the inside.

He discovered what he was looking for.

"Bobbi! Come here!" He pointed. Fastened just above the wide rear window and matching the upholstery so closely it was almost invisible, was a small electronic listening "bug".

"Quick, Lion! Take it down — "

"Shhh!" Lion's hand covered Bobbi's mouth.

She wriggled away. "Stop being funny!" Her voice was loud and angry. "What d'you think you're — "

"Shhh!" Lion said again, but this time he made no attempt to cover her mouth. Instead he took her arm and pulled her several steps away from the station wagon. Then in a voice that was scarcely more than a breath, he whispered, "Okay, now it's probably safe to talk. But quietly."

At last a look of understanding crossed Bobbi's face. She nodded, took another long look at the bug, then in a voice as soft as Lion's said, "It doesn't make sense. No one could have known we were going to be on this ferry because we didn't know it ourselves till we got here. They couldn't have planned ahead to catch the same one so they could use the time the cars were below decks to plant that bug."

"They could if they'd followed us from home," Lion said in a funny tight voice, remembering the red van that had refused to pass them. He told Bobbi what he was thinking. The worry came back into her eyes. She took hold of the station wagon door handle. "If I open this very quietly," she whispered, "you can take down the bug — "

Quickly Lion shook his head. He put his lips close to her ear. "Then they'll know we're on to them. If we want to find out what's going on and why they don't want Dad interfering in this case we've got to fool them into thinking we have no suspicions at all."

Bobbi moved back out of range of the bug. "You've read too many bad detective stories," she told him acidly. "But you're right about one thing. We can't take the bug down till after we show it to Dad."

"Show it to Dad?" Lion was so surprised he almost forgot to whisper. "I didn't think you were so chicken. You know how much Dad needed us to help him last time. Well, what if he needs us even more now? If we tell him about all this he'll put us on such a short leash we'll be lucky to get outside at all." The lines around his mouth softened. "Though, being grounded would solve my problems." He struggled not to grin. "Then you couldn't make me ride that dumb horse."

"Lion, be serious. You're saying we shouldn't say anything to Dad about the bug or about his briefcase?"

"Just for a little while. Just until we find out what's going on. You know Dad will never tell us — he's too worried we'll get hurt."

For the first time Bobbi smiled. "I guess he made that pretty clear with all that talk of staying out of things."

"And he's gonna need our help, Bobbi," Lion rushed on. "He's so busy worrying about his friend Jock and this old school friend that he's not even thinking about himself."

At that moment the loudspeaker on the wall beside them burst into life. "Attention please!" a metallic voice interrupted. "All passengers are now asked to return to their cars on the lower deck and prepare for disembarking at Langdale."

"That must be why that man wasn't keeping a more careful look out while he was rifling through Dad's briefcase," Bobbi said with sudden enlightenment. "He didn't expect anyone to come back below decks till after that announcement."

"Forget that man. Come on, Bobbi, stop stalling. Dad will be down here in just a minute." Lion glanced toward the stream of passengers already returning to the lower deck in response to the loudspeaker. "We don't have to keep quiet long. Just till we find out what's going on. Then we'll tell Dad everything."

Bobbi continued to frown. "He's going to see that bug as soon as he comes back to the car. Then how do we explain keeping quiet?"

"He won't see it because he won't be looking for it.

"Come on, Bobbi! Dad's thinking of everybody else but not himself. If he really is in danger like you said he might be, then it's gonna be up to us to help. And how can we help if we don't know what's going on?"

The resistance in Bobbi's frown softened slightly.

"Okay?" Lion prodded, watching the steadily growing stream of returning passengers.

At that moment Dad appeared at the bottom of the nearest staircase coming down from the upper deck.

"Please, Bobbi!" Lion urged again.

Dad started cutting through between the two parked cars right next to them.

At last Bobbi nodded.

"Remind me to send you the bill for my heart attack," Lion told her acidly.

"So, if everything's all right with the horses, we'll be on our way," Dad said cheerily. He didn't even glance into the back seat of the station wagon where the bug was sitting, but climbed behind the wheel and started the motor.

Lion felt a wave of relief. In fact, as they started to drive up the exit ramp he was feeling smugly pleased with himself. Then a momentary disruption behind them caught his attention. A vehicle from the outside lane seemed to be trying to edge into theirs. At first the other drivers resisted, then the car directly behind them let the new arrival in.

Lion's smug self-satisfaction evaporated. In fact, he suddenly found it hard to get enough air to breathe properly. For the vehicle that had pushed in directly behind them was a red van. The driver was tall and muscular looking, and he was wearing a faded jean jacket.

More than anything in the whole world Lion wanted to tell Bobbi — but how, with the bug directly behind him and Dad directly in front?

Chapter 6

They started along the winding coast highway and the red van followed.

Lion felt sick. He also felt scared. He kept wanting to look back at the bug, but he forced himself not to, for the red van was close enough that the driver might notice.

He looked over at Bobbi. Even without the added knowledge that the van was following, she was still as numb as he was. Ever since they'd got back in the car she'd been sitting in silence, staring rigidly ahead.

At last Dad noticed. "Is something wrong, honey?" he asked, glancing across the front seat.

Bobbi jumped as if her thoughts had been on something much different. "Pardon? — Oh, no — uh — nothing's wrong."

"Are you worried about the horses?"

"No — no — the horses are fine, Dad." Then to Lion's horror, she cast a quick look behind her at the bug before lapsing back into silence. If the receiver for the bug was in that red van, the driver would be listening to this dumb conversation, Lion realized. He'd have to be a complete idiot if he didn't catch on soon that something was suspicious, particularly after that glance of Bobbi's back at the bug. "Let's put a tape on," he suggested brightly. That was what spies on TV always did when they thought they were being bugged. "Something loud and cheerful, like that Heavy Metal one in the tray there." Leaning forward over the back of the seat he pointed.

"Could we negotiate a compromise?" Dad suggested. "How about the radio?" He turned it on, tuned in a country and western station and turned the volume down low. "Now," he went on, his voice no longer teasing, "perhaps one of you will tell me what's going on."

That would tell the listener for sure that they knew about the bug!

Resorting to the first thing that came to mind, Lion blurted in an overly innocent voice, "I've been trying to work out how far we've got to go and when you figure we'll get — " He broke off abruptly, and before Dad could answer substituted, "Though who cares." For he'd suddenly realized that if Dad said when they would reach Powell River the listener would know exactly what to plan to stop them! But he had to keep talking, so he said in a rush, "Actually, I'm feeling kind of sick." To be honest, that was more than half true. Ever since they'd started driving along this twisting coast highway he'd been feeling progressively greener, and people weren't expected to chatter normally if they were sick. "At least I know now why they say the Sunshine Coast is one of tourism's best kept secrets. It's not the sunshine and the scenery that's the secret — it's this road. If they ever let on what it's like nobody would ever come up here."

This time when Dad glanced back he was grinning. Had he stopped being suspicious? It wouldn't hurt to make sure, Lion decided, so he added brightly, "In about two more minutes I'm going to throw up."

"Then kindly put your head out the window."

"Come on Dad! I feel awful!"

"You've never been car sick in your life. You're the only person I know who can eat three hotdogs and a milkshake, then go on every ride at the PNE and feel great."

He'd succeeded in changing the direction of *Dad's*

thoughts, but now the *listener* would be even more suspicious!

"It's not just the curves and the swaying. It's the walls of giant trees bordering both sides of the highway," he rushed on. "It's like being shut in a narrow box with the sides constantly rushing past you." Actually, that much was true.

"I admit the trees are a bit claustrophobic," Dad agreed, glancing around. The amusement crept back into his voice. "But look on the bright side. If you should die of car-sickness you'd be famous — you'd make the Guiness Book of World Records. As far as I know no one else has died of car sickness yet."

Lion relaxed. At least for the moment, it seemed as if Dad had stopped being suspicious.

Gradually the curves began to space out a bit. Soon the road was swinging gently down to the water to the second ferry they had to catch, the one that ran from Earl's Cove to Saltery Bay.

The second ferry trip was as slow and boring as the first one. The only good thing was that there was no sign of the red van. Come to think of it, Lion reflected as they made good time after disembarking from the ferry, he hadn't seen the van for quite a while now. Not for the last few miles. Maybe it wasn't following any longer.

For the first time in what seemed like hours Lion relaxed. "So tell us about Powell River, okay Dad?" he suggested.

"It's an interesting place," Dad replied. "It's not only a major resort area, but it's the scuba diving capital of Canada."

Scuba diving! Great! Maybe he could do some scuba diving *and* catch international prawn thieves.

"It's also home to the largest octopus breeding

41

grounds in North America," Dad added, watching Lion in the rearview mirror.

Before he could stop them, shivers raced across Lion's shoulders. Quickly he turned away, for if Dad or Bobbi noticed, he'd be in for some major teasing. He couldn't help it. Snakes and spiders really bothered him. As for octopus! He'd better skip the scuba diving, he decided, and restrict himself strictly to chasing international prawn thieves.

"Apparently C.J. is even more of a scuba diving enthusiast than you," Dad was going on in the same innocent voice. "Perhaps we could ask him to lend you a wet suit and the two of you could dive down for a good close look at the octopus spawning grounds. I know that's something you wouldn't want to miss — "

He hadn't turned away quickly enough! Even Bobbi was laughing at him from the front seat.

Lion grinned sheepishly. "Great," he admitted, meeting first Dad's eyes and then his sister's.

That admission gave him a minute's breathing space, but he knew that if he didn't want to be roasted all the rest of the way to Powell River he had to change the direction of Dad's thoughts. So in the eager, inquiring tone that always worked when he was trying to distract teachers from things like undone homework, he said brightly, "Somebody said something about an underwater statue at Powell River."

"A bronze mermaid," Dad replied. "It's down near the wharf, and quite a tourist attraction I understand. Though as to how close it is to the octopus beds — "

Lion raised his eyes skyward in resignation. He should have known he couldn't con Dad.

Bobbi came to his rescue. "Hasn't Powell River also got a big pulp and paper industry?"

"Not only a big pulp and paper industry but also some of the finest fishing on the west coast."

"Which is why your friend Jock comes here, right?" Lion asked.

Dad nodded.

"But can they co-exist?" Bobbi put in. "Mightn't the pulp and paper industry pose problems for the fish stocks?"

"There are studies being done right now about that very thing," Dad answered. "Jock's report is among them. There is growing concern among a number of people that the effluent from the pulp mills can be harmful."

For the past few minutes Dad had been studying the shoreline. "I'm watching for Jock's favourite fishing spot," he explained. "It's just a little farther along here at a place called Garnet Rock. Since we have to pass directly by on our way to Mrs. Hamilton's, we'll stop, and if Jock is anywhere around we'll say hello."

The road was getting twisty again. For the next few minutes it demanded Dad's full attention, for many of the sharp curves had a dangerous fall-away on the outside edge.

Just as they were moving into one of the sharpest of the curves Lion had a vague impression of movement behind them. But he was too busy watching the twisting road to pay much attention. Then just as they reached the sharpest part of the outward curve, whoever was behind them accelerated, swung out and started to pass.

It was the red van.

There wasn't room! Already Dad had edged the station wagon and the horse trailer as far as he dared toward the right shoulder. He couldn't go any farther for at that point the edge of the road fell away in a steep drop.

The van continued to accelerate.

Dad had no choice but to move the car and horse-trailer over even farther.

Lion was too terrified to move. The weight and height of the horse trailer pulled them closer to the edge. As the wheels hit the uneven gravel surface of the shoulder he felt the horse trailer start rocking.

Dad fought for control.

Seemingly unaware of what was happening, the red van continued past without even a momentary break in speed, then disappeared around the curve ahead.

At least now Dad had some room to maneuver. Carefully he started to ease the car off the gravel and back onto the hard surface. To Lion's relief, as the wheels came back onto hard pavement the horse trailer stopped rocking. Still without touching the brakes, Dad continued to slow. Then finding a wide spot where it was safe to pull off, he stopped entirely and turned off the ignition.

"You'd better check those poor horses," he told Bobbi in a voice that didn't quite sound like his. "They're probably terrified."

Bobbi hurried to obey.

As she disappeared around the back of the trailer Dad opened his door and got out. "I'll just take a breather for a minute," he told Lion in the same funny voice.

Lion was too shaken himself to do more than nod. He watched as Dad moved a dozen paces down the gravel shoulder, then retraced his steps.

At the same time Bobbi reappeared from the back of the trailer. "They're looking a bit disgruntled — particularly Raj," she said with a grin, "but they're both fine."

Dad nodded. He waited for Bobbi to get in then got back behind the wheel. Starting the motor, he pulled back onto the highway. "I wish I'd taken that fellow's license number ..."

To Lion's relief it was Dad's own voice again.

" … Somebody needs to give that young man a stern talking to. His carelessness came very near to causing an accident."

All at once the terror Lion had felt when they'd almost gone over the edge of the cliff came rushing back. During the past few minutes he'd completely forgotten about the bug, but right this minute everything they were saying might be overheard. When the listener realized that his first plan to stop them had misfired, would he try again? A cold needle of fear settled somewhere deep in Lion's middle. Maybe he should have let Bobbi tell Dad about the bug and the man rifling his briefcase after all. Maybe this was too dangerous to try to sort out on their own.

But if Dad really was in danger, he'd need them to help, Lion reminded himself. If they told Dad what they suspected they wouldn't be able to help. Dad wouldn't believe them about there being any danger, accuse them of being melodramatic and imagining things, and pack them off on a succession of day-long sightseeing rides to keep them right out of everything. Or he would believe them that there was danger, and pack them off twice as quickly!

They had to wait at least a little longer before saying anything, he decided — at least till after they stopped to speak to Jock. Besides, nothing more could happen today. The van and the jean-jacket man had taken off, and they'd be in Powell River in a few more minutes. It wouldn't hurt to wait a bit longer and try to work things out. If by to-night, or first thing tomorrow, they still had no idea what was going on, then they'd tell Dad.

Chapter 7

Gradually the wall of trees on each side of the road began to thin. The road started to drop down and they emerged from the trees to find the highway running right alongside the ocean.

"There!" Dad said, slowing the car and pointing.

Lion pushed away his worries and relaxed at the beauty of the scene before them. Grey-blue waves rippled toward the rocky shoreline, each in turn rushing up, receding, then doubling under to make room for the next wave that was waiting. About a hundred yards out from the shore, and running parallel to it, lay a long narrow rock island, perhaps a third of a mile in length. "Garnet Rock," Dad said. "One of the most beautiful spots all up and down the Sunshine Coast, and a favourite spot for prawn fishing."

Even now several fishing boats were busy just a short distance beyond the island. One of the boats with two men on board was close enough for Lion to see clearly. The motor was idling so the boat was motionless, and the men seemed to be busy around some sort of winch at the boat's stern. "Why haven't they got any rods?" he asked.

"For prawn fishing you use traps," Dad told him, slowing to a stop and turning off the car motor so he could watch too. "The traps are filled with bait then lowered on thin steel cables."

"Lowered how far?"

"However far down the ocean floor is at that spot, because that's where prawn like to feed."

"So approximately how far down?"

"Anywhere from fifty feet to 350. As a rule the fishers put their baited traps down in the late afternoon, leave them overnight because that's when the prawn feed, then pull them up in the morning and see what they've got."

"Pull them up 350 feet?" Lion asked in surprise, still watching the men on the closest fishing boat.

Dad nodded.

"Don't any of them put on wet suits and dive down to check?"

"I shouldn't think so."

"Why not?" Lion protested. "It'd be way more fun."

"True," Dad replied, struggling to hide a smile. "But if there are prawns in the traps, as of course they hope there will be, they're going to have to pull the traps up to empty them, so they might as well do it first as last."

Lion had to admit that was a good point.

"Also," Dad went on, his attention no longer on the fishing boat but on Lion's reflection in the rearview mirror, "the same rocky areas and crevasses that attract the prawn for feeding also seem to attract the spawning octopus."

Again, before Lion could stop them, a series of shivers ran across his shoulders.

Bobbi burst out laughing.

Meeting Dad's glance, Lion made an invisible chalk mark in the air. He should have seen that coming.

"You called them fishers, not fishermen," Bobbi put in. "Do women fish for prawns too?"

"Lots of them do."

"Then how big are the traps?"

"The average would be about two feet in length by a foot wide and a foot high, made of a metal frame covered in mesh."

Bobbi looked stunned. "Two feet by one foot by one!

If one of those was filled with prawns how could anybody — man or woman — pull it back up to the surface through 350 feet of water!"

"With difficulty," Lion put in.

"With great difficulty," Dad agreed with a smile, "if they were to try to do it by hand. But today most of the fishers use electric winches." He nodded toward the boat closest to them. "That's what the men on that prawn boat are using. See the cable pulling tight across the deck? It probably has two prawn traps on the other end. Right now it's turned off because the men are lowering the traps into the water. There's no need to use the winch for that. Once the lock on the winch is released the weight of the traps plus the weight of the cable will pull them down to the ocean floor in seconds. But tomorrow morning when it's time to check those traps they'll need that winch to bring them to the surface."

Lion and Bobbi watched, fascinated.

Suddenly something went wrong. One of the fishers on the boat they were watching had slipped. They heard him yell, then watched in horror. One of his legs must have got caught in the cable that was unwinding rapidly across the deck. They could see him trying frantically to free himself, but the weight of the prawn traps on the other end held the cable taut. He was being dragged at an increasing speed across the deck. In the next instant he had been pulled overboard.

The other man on the boat seemed too stunned to do more than watch in horror as his partner disappeared under the surface of the water.

Dad was already out of the car. "Start the winch up the other way!" he yelled at the top of his lungs. "Pull him back up!" But he was too far away for his voice to carry. The second man continued to stand frozen.

48

A few seconds later the traps must have reached the ocean floor for the moving cable slowed and stopped, but there was no sign of the trapped man working himself free and breaking back to the surface. Nothing at all was moving on the water. In fact there was no longer any indication that anyone had even gone overboard.

Dad had started running the moment he left the car, and now Bobbi and Lion followed. "Start up the winch!" Dad called again. "There's still time to pull him back up!"

The other fisher still didn't seem to hear, or if he did, he was too stunned to react. But the motor of another boat had started up. It too had two men aboard. When it was close enough to where the first boat still sat motionless, one of the men dived overboard, holding what looked to Lion like a pair of metal cutters. Moments later the diver returned to the surface holding the injured man in his arms. Then rather than trying to get him back up on the fishing boat, he swam with him to shore.

Immediately Dad moved forward. He was close enough now to see the injured man clearly. "It's Jock!" he exclaimed in dismay.

At the sound of Dad's voice the injured man opened his eyes. A look of relief flooded his face. "Syd! … Knew I could … . count on you. … Need … a watchdog … Important …"

"Jock! What happened? Are you all right?"

But now the partner who had been standing frozen for so long had reached shore too, and before Jock could reply he said tersely, "I'm afraid I'll have to ask you to move out of the way. This man needs medical attention."

"But he's a friend of mine!"

"I can't help that. We've got to get him to a doctor." Deliberately Dad pushed past the other man and moved closer. "Are you all right, Jock?" he asked again. "There's some trouble of some sort, isn't there? Tell me what's going on —"

It was too late. Jock's eyes had closed and he'd lapsed into unconsciousness.

Someone must have radioed for an ambulance for the siren could be heard approaching. Moments later Jock was being taken away.

As Dad led the way back up to the highway where they'd left the car he was frowning and preoccupied.

"Do you think he's going to be all right?" Bobbi asked worriedly, moving up to walk beside him.

"I don't know. We'll stop at the hospital and find out." Dad was striding along so quickly Bobbi had to half run to keep up. "However, if I were Jock I'd get a more dependable buddy to fish with."

"What do you mean?" It was Bobbi's turn to sound frightened.

Dad slowed his pace and smiled over at her. "Pay no attention. I'm just over-reacting."

Lion, who had been following a dozen steps behind, felt a sudden jolt of fear. Maybe Dad *was* just over-reacting, but what if what had happened to Jock hadn't been an accident! What if it had been deliberately arranged!

The fear in Lion's middle changed to guilt. He should never have talked Bobbi into keeping quiet about the bug. If they'd told Dad, he'd have taken it out immediately. Then no one would have overheard Dad saying they'd stop and talk to Jock when they got to his favourite fishing spot. Because maybe that remark was behind both these near accidents — first their car being almost run off the road, now Dad's friend Jock being almost drowned. *What if somebody wanted to keep Dad and Jock from getting together?*

He had to tell Dad everything, Lion realized. It was too dangerous to keep quiet any longer. Sure, it would mean he and Bobbi got grounded, but that no longer mattered.

He started running to catch up. "Dad! Wait up a second, okay! There's something I've got to —"

The words ended abruptly, for Dad had reached the car and had opened the driver's door. Now as he turned back to listen to what Lion was saying he left the car door open.

Anything Lion told Dad now would be picked up on the bug!

"I've got — I've got to get a rock out of my shoe," he substituted lamely, bending down quickly to hide his expression.

For a moment there was startled silence, then Dad said at his driest, "I'm complimented that you feel you need me to supervise such a difficult operation. However, I've played along long enough. I think now it's time you explained just exactly what is going —"

"It wasn't because of the rock that I wanted you to stop," Lion interrupted quickly, frantically trying to think of a way to stop Dad from saying anything more while he was right beside that bug. "It's about the electric winch on that fishing boat." He clutched at the first thing that came to mind. "We studied about electric winches in school, and our teacher said nobody should use them except under really carefully controlled conditions." He continued a steady rambling argument about winches while he relaced his runner, watching Dad out of the corner of his eye.

"Do you think we can go now?" Dad asked in an even drier tone when Lion finally ran out of words. "Because I'd like to get to the hospital before much longer, if it's all right with you."

Lion knew Dad was too sharp not to be still suspicious, but for some reason he seemed to have decided to let it pass for the moment. Being grateful for small mercies, Lion followed Dad and Bobbi into the station wagon.

Then, to his surprise, after Dad pulled back onto the highway he didn't head straight for the hospital after all. Instead he turned away from the water and followed a road that curved sharply upward. When the road straightened out again, they were on a residential street that paralleled the highway. It too looked out at the ocean but from a half mile farther along and from much higher up.

"Is this where Mrs. Hamilton lives?" Bobbi asked, her attention not on the ocean but on the row of nicely kept residential homes with their rolling lawns and carefully tended gardens.

"No. Jock lives somewhere up here."

Don't say anything more about Jock! Lion willed silently. *Not till we're out of the car and away from that bug!*

Slowing the car, Dad started along the residential street, studying each house in turn. Half way along he stopped. "That's it." He pointed.

It was a white and brown ranch-style house set back from the street, surrounded by thick pine and cedar trees and a green rolling lawn. True, the grass needed cutting, but the lawn was richly green and the trees and shrubs were all neatly trimmed.

"He really cares about the look of his place, doesn't he?" Bobbi said, noting the spotless property. "No wonder he said he wanted a watchdog. He's probably afraid the place will be a mess if he's away too long."

Now Bobbi had forgotten about the bug!

"I rather suspect that Jock's request for a watchdog had more to do with himself than with his property," Dad replied dryly.

Don't say anything more!

"When we get to Mrs. Hamilton's I'll certainly phone

around and see if I can find some local person to come around and look after his property, but I'll personally take over the watchdog duties for Jock himself."

"So, are we going to the hospital now?" Lion asked.

"As soon as I check something."

Lion followed the direction of Dad's gaze. The view was the same as from the highway below, but because they were so much higher up it was much more detailed. He could still see the full expanse of Garnet Rock and the fishing boats lying at anchor, but now he could also see what lay beyond the island and off to each side.

He could also see the wharf itself, and all the people on it. Some were preparing to go off fishing, some were standing talking together in groups, others were just walking up and down. Out beyond the end of the wharf he could make out the shapes of several trawler boats, and farther out still a semi-circle of orange floats on the surface of the water marking the location of sunken prawn pots. He could even see any sightseers or saunterers who were wandering along this wide expanse of beach.

"I wonder why Jock made such a point about the view from his window," Dad said in a preoccupied voice, staring at the scene in front of him and speaking more to himself than to Lion or Bobbi.

Lion froze. *You'd be surprised how interesting the view can be from my window*, Jock had said in his note, and now Dad had just told that to the listener! It was too risky to let the silence go on any longer. In another minute Dad might say something more about Jock, or come out with something that was exactly what the listener wanted to hear. So blurting out the first thing he could think of Lion said brightly, "If someone with a house up here invested in a good pair of binoculars, I bet he could make his fortune as a gossip columnist."

"What a good idea!" Bobbi told him. She turned to Dad. "D'you think we could rent a room for Lion in one of these houses, then when we head back home he could stay and start his career?"

"It's a thought," Dad agreed, continuing to peer at the view. "He could pair gossip columnist with meteorologist. From here he should be able to come up with the right weather forecast just about every time." It was obvious Dad's thoughts weren't on the conversation but on the scene in front of him.

However, nonsense conversation was safer than lots of other things, Lion decided, so at his deliberate corniest he went on with feigned enlightenment, "Is *that* what a meteorologist does? I thought they had something to do with cleaning up space debris."

At that even Dad laughed.

Lion relaxed. Mission accomplished.

Coming out of his preoccupation Dad restarted the car. "Now we'll stop for a moment at the hospital, then go on to Mrs. Hamilton's."

Chapter 8

"When we get to Mrs. Hamilton's will C.J. be there?" Bobbi asked as Dad emerged from the hospital and rejoined them in the car.

"I'm sure he will," Dad told her. He smiled. "I hope you two get along. I have an idea that C.J. might need a friend. "

"What do you mean?"

Whatever the answer was, Lion didn't bother to listen. He hoped Dad and Bobbi would talk non-stop about C.J. all the way to Mrs. Hamilton's, because no listener was going to be interested in a Middle School principal or her fourteen-year-old son. And as soon as they got there and got out of the car so the bug couldn't pick up what he was saying, he was going to tell Dad everything.

But he couldn't talk to Dad for a while yet, he discovered, for as they drove up to Mrs. Hamilton's house an attractive dark haired woman was standing watching for them in the doorway.

"I was worried when you were so late," she told Dad as he unwound himself from behind the wheel. "I was afraid there might have been an accident or something."

Dad gave her a friendly hug and introduced Bobbi and Lion. "Actually there was an accident. In the water off Garnet Rock." He outlined what had happened. "The man pulled overboard was Jock McPherson. I think you know him."

"Of course! He's been doing a research report for our committee."

"I went to the hospital to try to find out how he was,

but the doctor was still with him so I couldn't go in. However, I'll check again in the morning."

"I hope he's all right." Mrs. Hamilton sounded worried. Then her face brightened. Including Bobbi and Lion in her glance as they too climbed out of the car she continued in an altogether different tone, "I'm so glad you've come, and C.J. will be too. I'll show you to your rooms so you can unpack, then we'll have dinner." Slipping her arm through Dad's she started piloting him toward the front door.

Bobbi moved after them.

Lion stayed by the car. "Can I stay out for a few minutes and stretch my legs?" he called, wishing Mrs. Hamilton would stop hanging onto Dad's arm. But that wasn't the reason he wanted to stay outside. He'd noticed someone standing in the shadows by the side of the house — watching them. About Bobbi's age, only taller and thinner with white-blond hair. In one arm he was carrying what looked like a bulky black wet suit, and in the other something else that was black and shiny, only Lion couldn't make out what it was.

"Certainly stay outside for a while if you wish," Mrs. Hamilton replied. She gave a quick glance up and down the street, then turned back to Dad and Bobbi. "I don't know where C.J. has disappeared to, but I'm sure he'll be back any minute. He knows you're coming and has been looking forward to meeting you." She continued toward the door. Then in an entirely different voice she admitted quietly, "I'm worried about him, Syd. That's why I'm so grateful to you for coming. I'm afraid he is far more frightened by all of this than he is letting on. I've tried to reassure him that no matter what happens, we'll — " The rest was lost as she opened the front door and led the way inside.

Lion turned back to the figure in the bushes. It was obviously C.J., for Lion could see his expression clearly, and no one but C.J. would have looked so murderous when Mrs. Hamilton said how much he was looking forward to meeting them.

Maybe this kid might not be so bad after all, he decided. In fact, maybe the two of them had a lot in common, because he'd have felt exactly the same way if he'd been in some kind of jam like C.J., and his mom had invited some unknown big city lawyer to come to straighten out his life.

He continued to wait. Sooner or later C.J. had to leave his hiding place and go join his mom in the house. And the minute he made a move in that direction, Lion was going over to talk to him. He'd tell him he knew just how he was feeling —

No, maybe on second thought that wasn't the thing to say — not when this guy was two years older. Better just to say hi, and then start talking about baseball, or —

C.J. was moving out of the bushes in the direction of the house.

Planning was forgotten. If Lion was going to reach the front walk at the same time as C.J., he had to start walking right now.

But C.J. had stopped abruptly. For a moment he stared toward the other side of the house, then he silently slipped back into the cover of the bushes.

Lion glanced over to see what C.J. had been staring at and realized with a shock that a second person was standing there. For a moment he had the vague feeling that it was someone he'd seen before, but even as the thought struck he pushed it away, for it was impossible. The figure then turned, sauntered casually back to the street, and strode away.

Quickly C.J. tucked the things he was carrying out of sight under a large lilac bush, then started after him.

Was that why C.J. hadn't let his mom know he was home? Because of that other person? Was that who C.J. had been waiting for? Lion watched the two disappearing figures. C.J. looked as if he was trying to catch up but the other man was moving too quickly.

Lion wished he could see more clearly, but all he could be sure of from that distance was that the man in front had lots of muscles and was wearing a faded jean jacket —

An icy emptiness opened up deep in Lion's middle. No wonder the guy had seemed familiar. The person C.J. was following was the van driver from the ferry.

Chapter 9

Now he not only had to find a chance to talk privately to Dad to tell him about the bug, Lion realized, he also had to find a chance to talk privately to Bobbi and tell her about C.J. and the van driver!

All through supper he tried to think of a way to do both things, with no success. Then, just as they were finishing the apple pie Mrs. Hamilton had made for dessert, the front door pushed open abruptly. "Sorry to be late," C.J. mumbled, coming into the room. He nodded as his mom introduced Dad, Bobbi and Lion, then sat down at the empty place at the table.

"I was worried about you," Mrs. Hamilton said simply, smiling across at him.

"Don't be silly, Mom," C.J. muttered, not meeting her glance. "I'm fine." He began rearranging the food on his plate.

For a moment it looked as if Mrs. Hamilton was going to say something more, but she must have thought better of it. In a completely different voice she said brightly, "After you've had your dinner, will you take Lion and Bobbi to the pasture next door and show them which gates to use for the riding trails?"

C.J. nodded without looking up.

"Your mother tells me there's a network of paths and logging roads around here that people can ride on," Dad put in. "Would you take Bobbi for a ride this evening and show her around?" He looked across at Bobbi and smiled. "After that long day in the trailer I think the horses could use a good run."

Lion sat back happily. He couldn't believe it! He was off the hook! Who cared if this guy was a nerd? From the way his sister was smiling it was clear she'd like nothing better than to ride out with C.J. all day every day. Which meant Lion could forget both riding and sightseeing. Now he didn't have to worry about getting hazed by all his friends when he got home for having spent all his time hanging around with his big sister. Instead, while C.J. and his sister were busy taking those dumb horses sightseeing, he could concentrate on fun things like —

Out of nowhere a new thought struck and he felt a rush of excitement. *Maybe while Bobbi and C.J. were sightseeing he could work out what was going on in that weird house-breaking scam*! Because Dad wasn't going to do anything about it — he'd told them that part was strictly police business. But someone had to work out what was going on, and if he could do it all on his own, Lion told himself, Dad and Bobbi would be really impressed!

The one hitch was that it would mean not saying anything to Dad about the bug or about his suspicions for a little while longer, and he'd decided after what happened this afternoon that he really should say something. But surely waiting just a day or two couldn't matter. Besides, now that they had reached Powell River there couldn't be much danger. As for the bug, how could it be a threat when nobody was spending much time in the station wagon now. And he wouldn't put off telling Dad for long — just till he'd had time to check out —

"I'm not really into horses or riding." C.J.'s voice interrupted Lion's daydream. The words were blunt, and an embarrassed flush had risen to his cheeks. "Besides, there's something I've got to do ... "

Something connected with whatever he had tucked under that lilac bush, Lion wondered?

"… But if you want to go right now I can take you over quickly and show you where to put your tack, and which pasture gate leads to the best trails."

"Your dinner!" Mrs. Hamilton protested, for he hadn't eaten more than a couple of mouthfuls.

No one paid any attention. Everyone was staring at C.J.

He'd been wrong in thinking they had anything in common, Lion decided. This guy was a nerd.

C.J. got to his feet. "Okay?" He started moving toward the door.

To Lion's amazement, Bobbi got up from the table and followed. She'd just been insulted and instead of being annoyed she looked as if she was feeling sorry for the jerk!

Well, Lion sure wasn't. He was boiling.

He followed C.J. and Bobbi through the hedge and into the pasture — he listened to what C.J. had to tell them about the various trails and gates and logging roads — then when C.J. was preparing to head back to the house, Lion moved up beside him. "So why didn't you let anybody know you were in the bushes outside when we first arrived?" he asked innocently.

C.J. was caught off guard. A mixture of guilt and surprise lit his blue eyes.

"And who's that big thug you tailed?" Lion's tone was no longer innocent.

C.J.'s face whitened. "What are you talking about?"

Lion was about to go on and say that the big thug in question had practically killed them on the way up, but he wasn't given a chance.

"Pay no attention to my dumb little brother," Bobbi interrupted cuttingly, moving between them.

Lion could have muzzled her. For a minute C.J. had looked as if he might have been startled into talking, but

61

Bobbi's intervention provided him with the time he needed to reconsider. Already the scared look had faded from his face. Ignoring Lion he turned back to Bobbi. "If you're clear on which trails to follow, I'll head back, okay? As I said, there's something I really need to do that I didn't have a chance to do earlier." Still ignoring Lion he gave Bobbi a quick smile, then headed back the way they had come.

Bobbi watched till he was out of sight, then she turned on Lion. "Way to go, lame brain. The poor guy was already upset — anybody could see that. He didn't need you sticking the knife in."

"But he's up to something! And whatever it is, it's connected with that van driver!"

"Ho, ho." Bobbi gave him a disgusted glare. "Dad's right. You really can't tell the difference any longer between the real world and B-grade television. What possible connection could there be between C.J. and that van driver?" Turning on her heel she set off back toward Mrs. Hamilton's driveway where the horse van was still standing.

"I don't know," Lion called after her. "I might have found out if you'd kept quiet a minute ago. But one thing I do know is that C.J. and the van driver know each other."

At that, Bobbi stopped walking and glanced back.

"When we first got here," Lion continued, "and you went into the house with Dad and Mrs. Hamilton, C.J. was hiding in the bushes by the side of the house. The van driver was watching from the bushes on the other side. When he took off, C.J. stashed the stuff he was carrying behind a bush and followed him."

Bobbi moved back toward him. "Are you serious?"

Lion nodded.

"What do you mean stashed his stuff? What stuff?"

"It looked like a wet suit and something else that was black and shiny. I don't know what. But I'll bet that's what he meant when he said there was something he needed to do that he didn't do earlier. I'll bet he wants to get back to move that stuff before somebody else sees it."

Bobbi's face creased into a frown. "It doesn't make sense. Why would C.J. follow the van driver?"

Abandoning his dreams of solving this all alone, Lion admitted his suspicions about their near accident on the highway.

For a long moment after he finished, Bobbi was silent. Then she turned and again began walking toward the horse trailer. "There's no way someone we don't even know would deliberately try to push us off the road." Her voice was scathing.

Lion moved after her. "Using that same logic, there's no way someone we don't even know would plant a bug in the station wagon and rifle Dad's briefcase."

Bobbi continued walking.

"Maybe," Lion added quietly, "you were right when you had that funny feeling about this case and said somebody was going to be in danger."

Bobbi stopped walking. She turned back. "So, what are you saying?"

Lion moved up beside her. "That I think somebody is in danger, only I don't know who. And I'm wondering if we should find out who it is before we say anything to Dad."

"But I thought you'd decided we should tell him."

"I had. In fact I tried to tell him right after Jock's accident — "

"That was what you were going to say when you came running up and then said you had a stone in your shoe!"

63

Lion grinned self-consciously. "I realized he was standing right by the bug with the car door open. How could I say anything then?"

Bobbi's look narrowed. "But now you've changed your mind?"

"Not about telling him," Lion said quickly, before his sister could insist they tell Dad right away. "I know we've got to tell him sometime. But I think we should hold off just for a little while."

"Why?" The word was blunt.

"Because things are starting to happen. Besides," Lion added, watching his sister without making it look too obvious, "I think we should find out first how far C.J. is involved."

From the look of surprise that crossed Bobbi's face it was obvious that hadn't occurred to her. "You mean you think he is involved just because you saw him following the van driver? That's crazy. Lots of people talk to lots of people. That doesn't mean they're working together!"

"Just the same, I think we should find out exactly where he stands before we say anything. What if this is all tied into that housebreaking scam? You know Dad said he wasn't going to get involved in that because it was police business. Well, if C.J. is already being set up somehow in that scam, what if this is tied in? What if C.J. is in some kind of trouble and needs help?"

For a long moment Bobbi was silent. Then she said thoughtfully, "So you're saying we shouldn't say anything about the bug because if we do, Dad will take it down."

"Mmm-hmm. Which will warn the guys behind this that we're suspicious, then they'll start being careful and we won't be able to find out anything."

Bobbi smiled. "Of course your decision has nothing to do with the fact that if we say anything Dad is sure to ground us — which will put an even quicker end to our hopes of finding out anything."

"That thought did occur to me," Lion conceded, matching her grin.

"Okay. I agree that we don't say anything for the moment."

Lion relaxed.

"Actually there's no way we can," Bobbi went on in an overly innocent voice. Turning, she started walking again toward the parked horse trailer. "We can't say anything at least till tomorrow morning because there's no time tonight. First we've got to unload our tack, take the horses for a run as Dad suggested, rub them down when we get back and give them some oats, then walk back to the house." The gleam of amusement in her eyes deepened. "By which time I bet Dad and Mrs. Hamilton will be deep in conversation about old times and won't even realize we're there."

C.J. and the van driver and Jock and everything else was forgotten. All Lion could think of was Mrs. Hamilton's arm tucked through Dad's as she led him toward the house, and Dad beaming down at her. "Maybe we should skip giving the horses a run," he suggested. "After all, since it's our first night here, we really should go back and be sociable."

Bobbi burst out laughing. "Stop worrying about Dad. He's a big boy now."

"I wasn't worrying about Dad!" Lion blustered. He turned away. He knew his sister had deliberately set him up. Even so, while they were out on the riding trails, images of Dad and Mrs. Hamilton flashed repeatedly into his mind. He was glad when they finally put the horses away and headed home.

As they reached Mrs. Hamilton's house, in spite of his

eagerness to play watchdog over Dad, he took a detour. Cutting across the lawn to the thick clump of bushes he checked underneath the lilac.

He'd been right about C.J.'s reference to "something he had to do." The wet suit and whatever else C.J. had put there had both disappeared.

Chapter 10

To Lion's relief, when he and Bobbi went back inside the house Dad and Mrs. Hamilton weren't alone. C.J. was with them. At the moment no one was talking, but obviously they had been, for C.J. looked defensive and sullen.

Lion wondered if anything had been said about C.J.'s behaviour earlier. But before there was a chance to find out, the doorbell rang.

Mrs. Hamilton went to answer it. She ushered a good-looking dark-haired man into the room. "This is Vern Rutner," she told Dad warmly. "He's one of the senior teachers at our school."

The newcomer shook hands, nodded a greeting at C.J., who had moved from where he had been sitting to a chair close to the door, and acknowledged Mrs. Hamilton's introduction of Bobbi and Lion. Then he turned back to Dad. "How was the trip? Long wait for the ferry? You were wise to catch the one you did from Horseshoe Bay." He sat down in the vacant chair opposite. "It can be a huge wait if you come over any later in the day."

It looked like it was going to be a long boring evening, so Lion joined C.J. near the door.

"Vern is one of my most outspoken supporters," Mrs. Hamilton went on, sitting down beside Dad and Mr. Rutner.

"She's got this silly idea that she's going to be replaced," Mr. Rutner explained, "but she's the best principal I've ever worked under."

C.J.'s expression tightened even more.

"Mr. Rutner sure seems to like your mom," Lion said in an undertone.

"You mean he'd like her to think he does. That's why he's laying it on so thick."

"Maybe he's afraid of losing his job," Lion suggested. "Maybe he's got money problems —"

"Rutner! The guy's loaded. He owns half the shares in the town's biggest industry."

At the bitterness in C.J.'s voice, Lion looked over sharply. But before he could ask anything more, C.J. got to his feet and slipped quietly out into the hall. A moment later he'd disappeared.

He'd obviously gone out, Lion decided. Actually, he didn't blame C.J. for being disgusted with the way Rutner was flattering his mom, but there was no point in getting on Rutner's case. Maybe all teachers tried to butter up their principals. Actually, they'd be dumb if they didn't.

He turned his attention to the living room. Rutner was continuing to beam at C.J.'s mom — but so was Dad!

A cold knot formed in Lion's stomach. For while Mrs. Hamilton was half ignoring Rutner, she was beaming right back at Dad! Could that be why she'd asked him up here? Were C.J.'s problems just an excuse to invite Dad for a visit?

All Lion's fears rushed back.

He wished they'd never heard of C.J. Tomorrow as soon as they made sure Jock was all right he was going to talk Dad into heading right back home.

But even as that thought registered, Lion felt a creeping sympathy for C.J. Maybe it wasn't all that long ago that his dad had decided to take off and do his own thing like Mom had. If so, Lion knew just how C.J. was feeling. Maybe, too, there wasn't all that much difference between being the kid of a Middle School principal or the kid of a famous criminal lawyer —

"Explain to me about this principal thing," Dad's voice broke into Lion's thoughts.

"I was appointed on a temporary contract two years ago when the proper principal was ill," Mrs. Hamilton replied. "Unfortunately his illness turned out to be more serious than anyone realized and last month he officially resigned. So the board has to hold a formal election to fill the vacancy."

"And Virginia is the logical choice," Mr. Rutner put in heartily. "It's nonsense to say she isn't good enough. She's a terrific influence for good in the community. Why, in addition to all her other work she's been spearheading a drive to prohibit the release of pulp mill effluent any-where near the fishing grounds."

Dad nodded thoughtfully. "I understand that can be quite a problem. My friend Jock McPherson has been heading up a government research team looking into the damage done to fish stock by the dioxin and furan in the effluent. In fact I have some test results with me that he wanted to see, but that will have to wait now till he's feel-ing better."

Quickly Lion glanced across the room at his sister. For the first time he remembered that conversation this morn-ing on the ferry. Bobbi had asked if there was anything valuable in his briefcase and Dad had said just a few briefs and a page of facts and figures. Were those facts and fig-ures the test results he was taking to Jock? Could that have been what the van driver had wanted to see? Could that also be why somebody had tried so hard this afternoon to keep Dad and Jock from talking to each other?

"You mean this research man is ill?" Mr. Rutner's words recalled Lion's thoughts.

"Some kind of fishing accident," Dad explained. "I was telling Virginia about it earlier. It happened just as we were arriving. We're hoping he hasn't been seriously injured."

"And that this accident won't mean his report will be delayed too long," Mrs. Hamilton put in, sounding worried.

Dad reached over and gently took her hand. "I suppose it could delay things for a while," Dad said, "but that shouldn't pose a serious problem." And he proceeded to explain why. Lion stopped listening. All he could think of was Dad taking Mrs. Hamilton's hand. Was that the sort of thing people did to casual acquaintances?

"Time you headed off to bed." Dad's voice broke into Lion's worries.

Gratefully he escaped back to his own room and crawled into bed. But it was impossible to fall asleep. Were Bobbi and Mr. Rutner still in the living room, he wondered? He hoped so. Every time he closed his eyes all he could see imprinted against the inside of his eyelids were images of Dad and Mrs. Hamilton laughing and joking together.

Chapter 11

Bobbi, Dad and Mrs. Hamilton were already at the breakfast table when Lion appeared next morning. In fact the others were almost finished. Bobbi was dressed for riding.

Dad looked up as Lion approached. "I've just been telling your sister that you two should take advantage of the glorious sunshine and go for a long ride to explore the area. While you're doing that, Mrs. Hamilton and I are going to the hospital. I phoned first thing this morning and they say Jock is out of danger but is still not allowed visitors. So I want to speak to the doctor. Then we have an appointment at the police station to talk to some of the officers who have been involved in this strange housebreaking scam that I told you about."

Lion had been busy deciding whether to have raisin bran or frosted flakes for his breakfast, but at this he looked up sharply.

"So far nothing has been made public," Dad went on, "but it's clear some of the young people are involved, so Mrs. Hamilton has asked to speak to the officers." He grimaced wryly. "They probably won't tell us much but at least they have agreed to talk." Dad got to his feet and moved toward the door.

Mrs. Hamilton got up from the table too, and started to follow. Then she stopped and turned back. "I'm glad you two are along," she said simply, smiling at them. "Be patient with C.J. He's having a bad time right now." For a second it seemed to Lion that there was a glimmer of tears in her eyes, but he couldn't be sure, for with another smile she turned away.

"So eat your breakfast and let's go riding," Bobbi said before Lion could think of a reason why he should go running after Dad and Mrs. Hamilton and beg to go with them. At the same moment C.J. appeared in the doorway. "Did you say you were going riding?" he asked, moving toward the table.

Lion glanced around in surprise. Had C.J. heard Dad say they were going to the police station? He had a suspicion the answer was yes, for a funny defensive look had come into C.J.'s eyes. But when he spoke his voice was positively friendly and his lips were smiling. It was the first time since they had arrived that Lion had seen him do anything but scowl!

"If it's okay with you, maybe I'll come along."

Lion stared in amazement. What had happened to the "not into horses" bit?

"It's a long time since I've done any riding," C.J. went on. "Maybe I'll get you to give me a few pointers before you head off."

Bobbi beamed delightedly. "I'll start right now while you have your breakfast." And she launched into a cheery sales pitch about all the things that were great about horses and riding.

Lion had decided on Frosted Flakes. Ignoring Bobbi's sales pitch he watched C.J. from under half-lowered lids as he filled his cereal bowl. Why the sudden about-face? What was C.J. planning? The trouble was he couldn't even guess. In which case he might as well eat, he decided. Still ignoring his sister's chatter, he started in.

But before he'd taken more than two mouthfuls it occurred to him that C.J. was ignoring his sister's chatter too. He'd spread marmalade on his toast but he wasn't eating it. And from the frown between his eyes it was obvious he was thinking of something else entirely.

Then why had he suddenly said he'd come riding? That bit about being interested in learning pointers must be a lot of garbage. If C.J. was interested in pointers he'd be listening to Bobbi right now. Was he planning a meeting with the van driver? Or was he just pretending to be going with them as an excuse to get out of the house? But why bother with an excuse when his mom had already left?

Lion continued working on his Frosted Flakes.

"Okay?" Bobbi asked both of them as Lion took his final mouthful, for C.J. had finished his toast despite his preoccupation.

C.J.'s attention came back. Almost unconsciously, it seemed, he glanced at his watch, then got to his feet. "Okay," he agreed.

Lion followed them to the pasture Mrs. Hamilton had arranged for them to use.

"Don't worry about me," C.J. was saying. "Just go ahead and do what you always do. I'll just watch."

"Watching isn't enough," Bobbi told him. "If it's been a long time since you've ridden, you'd better have a review of the basics. So while I explain, Lion will demonstrate. Then it'll be your turn to get up and try."

Lion had been only half listening, but now his attention snapped back. "What's to demonstrate?" he protested. "You can tell him what to do and he can do it straight off. You don't need me to play middle man. There's no trick to riding a dumb horse."

"It'd help if I could watch you first." C.J. said in a deceptively mild tone. Again he glanced at his watch.

Lion was more convinced than ever that C.J. was up to something, and he was just about to refuse to have any part of this demonstration business when it occurred to him that this might be his chance to prove he wasn't just

Bobbi's useless little brother, as C.J. seemed to think. At least, it'd be his chance to prove it if his horse would co-operate.

He helped Bobbi groom and saddle both horses, then leading Raj a little distance away, moved close to the big horse's head and eyeballed him closely. In a voice he knew wouldn't carry over the conversation still going on between Bobbi and C.J. he muttered darkly, "Okay, hotshot, let's do it right for a change, okay?"

Raj gave him an innocent stare.

Lion wasn't fooled. He climbed aboard then closed both knees in a death grip on the saddle leathers and prepared for Raj to roll his back and take off at a gallop.

Instead the big bay gelding lifted his head, moved up on the bit, then started off at a sedate walk around the enclosed pasture.

He had to be sick, Lion decided as they completed the circle. He was just about to tell Raj so when Bobbi called, "He's going so nicely, why don't you put him over that log and let C.J. see him jump?" She pointed to a smooth fallen tree that lay in a clear area of grass.

Lion kept Raj moving the other way. "Don't be funny."

"There are no rocks around, or any gopher holes," Bobbi called as if Lion hadn't spoken. "It's the perfect spot to see what he can do."

"No way." Then to make sure his sister heard he turned Raj around and headed back toward her. "No way." he repeated. "It's too much of a temptation."

Bobbi looked puzzled. "For you?"

"For him. I know how his mind works. He'll pretend he's going to jump, wait till I move forward off the saddle, then at the last minute put on the brakes and dump me."

"Not if you think him over."

"End of joke," Lion told her moving on again.

"I'm not joking," Bobbi called after him. "All you've got to do is picture in your mind what you want to do. Look over top of that log to the pasture beyond as if that's where you know the two of you are going. Raj will feel what you're thinking and he'll do it."

"This is Raj you're talking about, not Big Ben."

"Try it and see. It's called empathy."

"No." Lion and Raj continued down the field.

Bobbi raised her voice louder. "It happens all the time between a horse and rider."

"Not between this horse and this rider."

"Just think about what you're going to do and look in that direction. Raj will sense what you want and go along with it."

Lion had no intention of having any part of that ridiculous scheme. Then he noticed C.J. watching, an expectant grin on his face. He realized with dismay that if he refused to jump, C.J. would think he was scared!

Again he turned Raj back toward his sister. "Are you serious about this empathy stuff?" he asked in an undertone when he was close enough to be heard without yelling.

"Try it."

"Will you pick up the pieces if I get dumped?"

"You won't get dumped. Just don't look at the log. Look over it to the field on the other side and think him there."

Lion saw C.J.'s grin broaden. He had to go through with it now, he realized. Leaning forward in the saddle till his head was close to Raj's, he whispered fiercely, "You heard what she said about that empathy stuff. No games, okay? If you put on the brakes — " He left the rest of the threat unspoken. Feeling like a cavalryman riding to almost certain death at the charge of the Light Brigade, he put Raj into a canter and headed for the fallen log.

To his amazement, Raj jumped. Not gracefully. He took off too soon, jumped way higher than he needed to, and landed with such a rough jolt that Lion lost both stirrups — but he cleared the tree.

Surprise replaced the expectant grin on C.J.'s face. "Hey! How about that!" Lion exclaimed. There was nothing to this jumping business after all. He was so pleased with himself he was just about to say he'd put Raj over something much higher when the big horse took off across the field in a stiff-legged gallop, tossing his head and rolling his back.

"Cut it out!" Lion yelled, struggling not to fall off with each jarring step.

Raj galloped faster.

Lion pulled back on the reins with every ounce of energy he could muster. "Whoa!" he thundered.

Raj slammed on the brakes.

Lion sailed over his head, landing in a heap on the pasture grass.

"That's the last time I ever jump this horse," he muttered as Bobbi came running up to see if he was still alive. He brushed the dirt out of his mouth with the back of one hand.

"He was just obeying orders," Bobbi protested. "You told him whoa."

Lion threw her a glance full of loathing. Pretending he didn't know C.J. was laughing, he began a check to make sure nothing was broken. "So much for you and your empathy."

"How d'you know this wasn't empathy?"

"Funny, funny." Since everything still seemed to work, he got painfully to his feet.

"I'm serious. You've got to admit you were feeling pretty proud of yourself after you took that jump. How do you know Raj didn't sense what you were feeling and decide to show you he felt the same. Running off would be the logical way for him to show it. But then you hollered so loud at him to stop that he realized you were mad so he put on the brakes."

Lion was speechless. How could his sister utter such nonsense and sound as if she meant it! Then he realized that maybe she did. Why did she have to say anything at all? Why couldn't she have just left it? Darn it all, now he'd never know for sure whether Raj had dumped him on purpose or not.

He stole a glance at C.J. to see if he was still laughing, but C.J. was no longer even looking in their direction. He'd moved to a small raised knoll near the top of the pasture and was standing staring towards the street.

Raj and empathy were forgotten. Quickly Lion moved closer to see what was holding C.J.'s attention. From the small knoll he had an unobstructed view of the street.

Was that why he'd agreed to come with them and had been checking his watch so carefully? So he could slip away without anyone suspecting that he was waiting for someone?

What if it was the red-van driver?

The thought came out of nowhere and Lion wished it would go away again equally quickly. If that was who C.J. was watching for —

"I've got to leave for a second," C.J. called across the pasture to Bobbi. "I'm really sorry but there's somebody I've got to speak to. However, I won't be long. As soon as I get back you guys can show me some more —" The rest was lost as he hurried away.

"I'm going to see what he's up to," Lion said quickly.

"No!" Bobbi protested.

"I won't be long. Just a few minutes. Will you catch Raj so he doesn't snap his reins running around with them dangling?" Without waiting for his sister to answer he started after C.J.

By the time he reached the street C.J. was a block ahead, *and a dozen paces ahead of him was the van driver*! Lion swung in behind. He wondered why C.J. didn't run if he wanted to catch up, but maybe he didn't want to. Maybe he was just following. Well, two could play at that game, Lion decided. If he followed too and found out where they were going he might be able to work out what was going on.

But when he reached the next intersection and rounded the corner both of them had disappeared. Lion stopped in confusion. He hurried down the block, looking for any lanes, or spaces between buildings, but there was no sign of either C.J. or the van driver.

Now which way should he go? Slowly he glanced around in a complete circle. Then the prickles started running down his spine. *For now he was the one being followed!* There was still no sign of C.J. but the van driver was behind him and less than half a block away. Lion could see all those muscles rippling across his arms and shoulders.

Why had he ever thought it was important to find out where C.J. was going or what he was involved in? It wasn't his business. If C.J. and the van driver were friends that was fine. He wouldn't get in their way. He'd just head off home.

At the next intersection he turned at right angles to the direction he had been taking.

The van driver turned at right angles too.

A tight band formed around Lion's chest as the distance between himself and the man behind became shorter.

Lion walked faster.

So did the man behind.

It suddenly occurred to Lion that maybe he should have told Dad what was going on after all! Now it could be too late! Being a big hotshot hero and working out what was going on was fine so long as he didn't end up dead doing it! He should never have got involved in this case in the first place. He should have trusted his sister's feelings. Well, next time —

Only chances were good there wouldn't be a next time, because the guy behind was steadily gaining. Lion knew he couldn't outrun him — he'd discovered that on the ferry.

He looked around frantically.

Directly ahead at the intersection a harassed mother was struggling to get across on the "walk" light, taking with her an armload of groceries, a baby in a stroller, a leashed dog, and a young toddler.

Lion saw his chance. "Can I help?" he asked moving up beside her, hoping his voice didn't sound as scared as he felt.

Gratefully she handed him the leash and the groceries. At the opposite curb she reached out to take them back but Lion shook his head. "I'm going this way too," he told her. Confident he'd outsmarted the man in the jean jacket he glanced backward.

The man from the ferry was still following. He felt a wave of panic, for the man would probably keep following till they reached where the lady lived, and then what?

The panic grew worse. Then Lion had an idea. Again he looked backward, but this time he made no attempt to be secretive about it. "There's a man behind us," he said in a loud innocent voice that he knew would carry. "Is it somebody you know?"

At that the lady turned and looked carefully at the man in the jean jacket. "No, I don't think so."

"Then I wonder why he's following us," Lion said in the same clear voice. "When we get to your place I'd better phone Dad and describe the guy to him. He could be planning to help himself to your groceries or something."

"Oh, dear!" Again the lady looked back obviously upset. But the next moment she was smiling. "It's all right. He's not following us after all. He's turned down that other street."

The relief was so great it was all Lion could do not to drop the groceries. But then his shivers came back. Why had the man been following him? Because he'd been following C.J., or was there another reason? Maybe he'd outsmarted the guy this time, but what if he came back?

Chapter 12

By the time Lion got back to the pasture Bobbi was really worried. "What happened? Where have you been? I was afraid something must have happened!"

"It almost did," Lion confessed with a grin, for now that he was safely back he could joke about it. "You know how on TV when somebody tails somebody else it looks easy? Well, that's smoke and mirrors. Real life is different." And he told her about thinking he was following C.J. only to discover that C.J. had suddenly disappeared and the van driver was following him!

"The van driver! Why would he follow you? What did he want?"

"I didn't wait to find out." And he told her about the lady and her groceries.

For the first time Bobbi laughed. Then her face sobered. "You said C.J. disappeared. Did he disappear before or after you noticed the van driver?"

"After. But C.J. didn't know I was following."

"Then C.J. can't have had anything to do with someone following you," Bobbi said with relief.

Until then that thought hadn't occurred to Lion. Maybe Bobbi was right. On the other hand, maybe his sister was looking for excuses because she liked C.J. —

Lion's thoughts ended abruptly. The person he'd been thinking about had reappeared on the far side of the pasture.

"Sorry to take off that way," C.J. called, starting across the pasture at a run toward Bobbi. Suddenly he stopped, clearly surprised at seeing Lion behind her.

C.J. wouldn't have been able to see him sooner because he'd been hidden by Bobbi and the horses, Lion realized. So was the surprise just disappointment because he'd been hoping to have Bobbi's undivided attention, or was the surprise shock because he hadn't expected Lion to come back! The fear that had corkscrewed deep in Lion's middle when the van driver had been closing in on him, came back. Was Bobbi wrong? Had C.J. known the van driver was tailing him? Had something more been planned than just tailing?

"So now it's your turn to ride," Bobbi called to C.J. as he started again toward them. "Lion will give you a leg up on Raj and I'll ride with you on Brie." As she spoke Bobbi turned and tightened Brie's girth.

Lion expected C.J. to refuse. Instead he seemed quite willing. What was he up to now, Lion wondered? Why the sudden about-face? Was he using the riding lesson as an excuse for hanging around, because he liked Bobbi? If that was all, then he could go home and watch TV reruns, Lion decided. But what if C.J. was hanging around because he expected the van driver to come back?

He'd stick around. There was no way he was deserting his sister if jean jacket might be coming back.

He gave C.J. the leg-up his sister had requested, and adjusted his stirrup length, then moved over to a bale of alfalfa hay and perched on the edge. "So this time you demonstrate and I'll watch," he told C.J.

His sister gave him a quick grateful glance.

With a start Lion realized that she'd been afraid he might leave and hadn't wanted him to! She'd wanted him to stay! He felt a warm cosy glow somewhere deep inside.

From the soft smiley look that came into his sister's eyes he realized she'd guessed how he was feeling! What if she made fun of him! What if she made some joke to C.J.!

A thing like that could be really embarrassing —

But she'd guessed how he felt about that too. With another quick smile she turned away. She repeated a quick rundown of riding essentials, sounding business-like, matter-of-fact and completely unemotional, and Lion's insides settled back into place.

C.J. settled his feet into the stirrups and gripped the reins in rigid fingers. If he'd done some riding years ago, it must have been a whole lot of years ago, Lion decided, and he settled back to enjoy himself.

So far Raj continued to stand motionless, looking as if he didn't even know he had a rider on his back.

"Give him a good firm kick with your heels," Bobbi directed.

For the first time in ages Lion found himself grinning. He hadn't forgotten the first time he'd ridden Raj, and the wild ride he'd had after Bobbi had given him those same instructions. If C.J. had deliberately set him up for that scare from the van driver, then maybe this was his chance to get even. Settling himself more comfortably on the bale of alfalfa he waited expectantly.

C.J. shifted one hand from the reins to the saddle horn. His knuckles whitened.

Raj continued to stand motionless.

"Go ahead. Use your heels," Bobbi urged.

Again Lion waited expectantly.

C.J. moved his legs out from the saddle leathers and slapped hard with both heels against the big horse's flanks.

Raj's head came up. Lion could see the wheels turning. Then, to his disgust, Raj moved forward at a sedate walk that wouldn't have frightened a baby.

"Good!" Bobbi applauded.

Lion couldn't believe it. Had Raj seen him watching?

Was that the reason he was being so obliging? To show him up and make him feel like a fool?

C.J. took Raj in a complete circle around the pasture and arrived back to where Bobbi was waiting.

"Good," Bobbi said again. "I'll go with you this time." They moved off together around the pasture.

Again Lion waited for something to happen. Instead his sister and C.J. made their way around the pasture laughing and joking as if they were really enjoying themselves.

"Now let's try it at a trot," Bobbi suggested as they started on the third round.

Surely now there'd be some fun, Lion told himself. No way Raj was going to put up with somebody bumping and jarring up and down on his back with every step.

But Raj continued to behave beautifully.

Lion couldn't believe it. They'd come up here to play the Three Musketeers and right the wrongs of the world, and now suddenly everybody seemed to have forgotten all about that. Dad seemed to want to spend all his time with Mrs. Hamilton — his sister wanted to spend all her time with C.J. — and even Raj who he'd brought along specially so they could chase international prawn thieves had made it clear he preferred C.J. to him!

At last Bobbi and C.J. completed their third circuit around the pasture and brought the horses to a stand. Swinging to the ground, C.J. handed Raj's reins to Lion.

"Thanks," he said simply. "He's a great horse. Now I'd better get back to the house. There are a couple of jobs I promised Mom I'd do." He went striding back across the pasture in the direction of the house.

Lion was still feeling too hurt and ignored by everybody to do more than nod. In silence he watched C.J. go, and was just debating whether he'd take off too when he was pushed off balance by Raj's head rubbing hard against his chest. "Hey! Cut it out!"

Again Raj rubbed his head roughly up and down. Then he straightened, snorted through his nostrils, gave his whole body a shake, and turned his attention to seeing if there was any edible grass nearby.

Had he done that on purpose, Lion wondered? Had Raj sensed how left out he'd been feeling? But that was craziness, he told himself brusquely. He was getting as bad as Bobbi. As he'd told her dozens of times, horses weren't human. They didn't sense things like that. The big lug's face had probably been itchy from the bridle and he'd decided Lion's chest was the handiest place to scratch it.

That was all.

With that settled, he took off Raj's saddle and set to work rubbing him down.

Bobbi had unsaddled Brie and was grooming her as well. For a few minutes she worked in silence, obviously doing some thinking for her face had clouded. At last she said thoughtfully, "You keep assuming that C.J. and the van driver are working together, but you said that C.J. didn't know you were following him."

"True," Lion admitted.

"And you said that he didn't see the van driver following you because he'd turned off before then."

That was true, too, Lion admitted.

"So the chances are good that he *didn't* know the van driver was following you," Bobbi went on. "But if he *did* know, then the reason he turned off without trying to help must be because he's scared of the van driver."

Lion didn't argue, for that thought had occurred to him too. "Which means the van driver must be connected somehow with the trouble C.J. is in about this housebreaking business."

It was Bobbi's turn to nod. The worry in her face deepened. "C.J. would never deliberately do anything to hurt anybody," she said softly. "I know he wouldn't. He's a really nice guy." For a moment she looked down, studying the toe of her riding boot, then in an even lower voice she added, "If C.J. is in trouble, Lion, we've got to help."

Chapter 13

The smell of freshly baked cookies greeted them as they walked in. "Dad and Mrs. Hamilton must be back," Bobbi remarked. "I wonder how Jock is doing, and if they were allowed to see him?"

"I wonder. And if they found out anything from the police."

"Let's go ask."

"What a dreamer," Lion told her scathingly. "Do you think they'd tell us if they had found out anything?"

"No, probably not."

"So forget the police. Let's concentrate on talking Mrs. Hamilton into giving us some of those cookies."

Bobbi smiled. "All right. Only first, you'd better make peace with C.J." She nodded toward his bedroom. They could hear him moving around inside.

Maybe he had been a bit hard on C.J., Lion decided, and he moved toward C.J.'s door. But just as he raised his hand to knock, it pushed open from the other side.

"Oh!" Lion backed away in confusion. "Sorry. I was looking for C.J."

"You just missed him," Mr. Rutner replied heartily, coming out through the open doorway. "He left about fifteen minutes ago. He'd only just come back in — said he'd been down at the pasture with you two. Then the phone rang. It was his boss calling him in for a work shift." His smile widened. "I figured while he was out would be a good time for me to look after that broken light socket in his room that he's been wanting me to fix."

For a minute Lion was surprised that C.J. would ask

Mr. Rutner for a favour when he seemed to dislike him so much. Then he realized it was probably C.J.s way of trying to make up for being unfriendly last night. He gave C.J. full marks. He hoped he'd be as generous if someday he ended up in C.J.'s position —

He suddenly realized that Rutner was watching him, an amused expression on his face. Had Rutner guessed what he'd been thinking? Quickly he forced a bright interested look. "Does C.J. work on the prawn traps every day?"

"No. Just when he's called. There's quite a number of kids on the list. They're called in rotation." Mr. Rutner brushed past Lion and started along the hall.

"Is it hard work?" Lion asked, moving after him.

"It's heavy and tiring. Also the kids have to be pretty good swimmers and divers. If cables get tangled, or prawn traps get stuck, it means diving down in pretty deep water to fix whatever is wrong."

Lion was about to ask more questions about the wharf job when Mrs. Hamilton called from the living room, "If you've finished with whatever you're doing, Vern, would you come in here next?"

"I'd better go," Rutner told Lion with a grin. He nodded at the tool kit he was carrying. "Being an Electronics Shop instructor has its uses. Next on the list I think is a broken window catch." Raising his voice he called, "Mr. Fix-it! On the way!" He moved past Lion and down the hall.

It was Lion's turn to grin as he watched him disappear. Maybe he wasn't going to have to worry about having a Middle School principal for a stepmother after all. Dad couldn't fix a broken light socket or a window catch if his life depended on it.

Brushing his hands against each other as if to dislodge invisible crumbs, Lion set off to find Dad. Maybe Bobbi was right and they should at least see if Dad would tell them what happened at police headquarters. Maybe if Lion asked the right questions ...

Locating Mrs. Hamilton, he asked her where Dad was.

"Downtown," she replied. "After we left the hospital there were some other things he wanted to do."

"Did they let him see Jock?"

Mrs. Hamilton shook her head. "Tomorrow, they said." She tucked some papers she had been reading into her briefcase. "I'm going to be leaving in just a few minutes to go downtown to meet him, so do you want me to ask him to phone you? I don't think we'll be back much before dinner."

There was no way he could talk Dad into telling him anything over the phone. So answering Mrs. Hamilton with a polite "No thanks," he went in search of Bobbi.

He found her eating cookies.

He explained about Dad. "So, d'you want to go sight-seeing?"

Bobbi gave him a disbelieving stare. "Since when have you become interested in sightseeing?" The words were muffled by cookies.

"Since it occurred to me that somebody has got to try to work out exactly what's going on here, and since Dad doesn't seem to be doing much, we'd better."

Bobbi's eyebrows lifted questioningly.

"As somebody else once said," Lion added, "sightseeing is a foolproof cover for meeting lots of people and asking lots of nosy questions."

Bobbi burst out laughing as her own words from a few days ago were thrown back at her. Licking her forefinger she lodged a sticky invisible score in the air. "Where do you want to sightsee?"

"At the wharf."

"The wharf? Why?"

"Because I think that's where C.J.'s gone."

Instantly Bobbi's face brightened.

Lion pretended he didn't notice.

"Are you sure you know how to get there?" Bobbi asked, "because I don't."

"I know you don't," Lion agreed. It was a standing family joke that she had absolutely no sense of direction. "But I do, so trust me."

Ten minutes later, after cutting through several side streets, down one hill and up another, he brought them out on the residential street just above the ocean that Dad had driven along yesterday. Directly below stretched the ocean with swell after swell of grey-blue waves rolling gently in against the rocky shoreline. "There's the wharf just down there." He pointed.

Bobbi wasn't even listening. She was turned the other way staring at the house they'd just passed — a gabled white and brown ranch-style house set back from the street, surrounded by thick pine and cedar trees and a green rolling lawn. It was Jock's house. "Look, Lion! Dad's got a gardener working there already!"

Lion looked where she was pointing. A man in jeans was pushing a lawnmower over the immaculate green lawn. "Well, you've got to say one thing for Dad," Lion joked. "When he says he'll arrange for a gardener, he doesn't waste any time,"

"We'd better tell him at supper."

Lion's eyebrows lifted. "That he doesn't waste time?"

"No, silly. That the gardener he arranged for has come and is already working." She turned back to study the wharf.

"Let's go closer," Lion suggested. "We can see everything a lot better if we go right down there." As he spoke he led the way back down to ocean level. Now they could see all the activity up and down the wharf and also what was going on in the water close by. A number of fishing boats had been moored alongside the wharf and their owners were busy stowing supplies and gear on board. Other boats were anchored just a short distance out with fishermen hauling up their traps to check their take. On the wharf itself more than a dozen teenagers were working, some attaching cables to large rectangular mesh prawn traps, others taking bait from large containers and filling small clear plastic bait cans.

"There's C.J.!" Bobbi exclaimed delightedly, pointing to a figure at the far end of the dock. "What's he doing in a wet suit?"

Quickly Lion looked where Bobbi was pointing. Sure enough, C.J. was leaning over the end of the dock pulling on a cable, dressed in a wet suit.

"Let's go closer and watch," Bobbi suggested, moving forward as she spoke.

But Lion caught her arm. "First, let's make sure jean jacket isn't lurking around watching." Carefully he studied each group on the wharf, looking for anyone who even vaguely resembled the van driver. There was no sign of him. But now something else had caught his attention. "Listen," he said.

Voices were carrying easily from the end of the wharf as voices do near water. "Tattle-tale!" someone said acidly.

"No, a momma's boy!" someone else corrected.

C.J. had ducked his head and was concentrating on the cable as if it was the most important thing in the world.

"Found any more tales to carry home?" a third voice asked.

"Of course he has. He's gotta squeal on somebody. That's how he keeps his momma happy."

"We don't like spies around here."

The angry remarks continued.

Lion glanced at Bobbi. She was clearly upset. Lion wasn't quite sure where his own sympathies lay. If the remarks were true and C.J. had been carrying tales home to the principal, then he deserved to have the kids on his case. Didn't he realize how dumb that was?

He was about to say so, when Bobbi said abruptly, "I'll be right back." She moved away.

"Where are you going?"

Bobbi didn't answer.

"Bobbi! Come back!" Lion called in a half whisper.

Still without answering, Bobbi tucked her hands in her pockets, then adopted a casual air and started down the wharf. When she was about half way along she called cheerily, "Hi, C.J.! What are you doing?"

Startled, C.J. glanced up.

"Need some help with that cable?"

The wharf grew suddenly silent. The kids who a second before had been yelling jibes were staring at Bobbi.

C.J.'s face flushed with embarrassment. He looked first at Bobbi, then at the other kids, guessing that she must have heard what they had been saying. "No, it's okay," he replied and turned away.

Bobbi continued her casual saunter.

As Lion watched he felt the prickles starting across his shoulders. What did Bobbi think she was doing! Didn't she know how dumb it was to deliberately taunt a whole gang of kids? Particularly when they were all friends and she was a stranger!

She continued walking. Now she had closed the distance between herself and C.J. to a couple of dozen paces.

"I'd be glad to help!" she called again. "If you just show me what you want me to — "

The words ended abruptly as two older teenagers stepped in front of her blocking her way. "Thanks, but he doesn't need any help," one of them said coldly. "Didn't you hear him say that? So maybe you should mosey on before you get hurt. This is no place for girls."

At that Lion moved forward. Sure, Bobbi was being dumb, but she was doing it in a good cause. There was no way he was going to stand back and let those two goons scare his sister.

But Bobbi wasn't scared. Or if she was, she didn't let on. She beamed back at the teen who'd spoken with her sunniest smile. "It's really nice of you to be concerned, but I won't get hurt." While he was still trying to recover she moved past him and continued walking.

Lion's heart, which had stopped beating altogether for a minute, started up again. It was all he could do not to laugh. Two guys twice her weight and strength and at least four years older, and she stops them cold by playing innocent! But he knew they'd soon recover. And before they did, he had to get her out of there, because two guys that age weren't going to sit back and let some girl make fools of them. "Come on, Bobbi!" he called. "Let's go!"

She glanced back and waved, but made no move to retrace her steps. Instead she continued down the wharf. "I'd be glad to help," she called again, continuing to move toward C.J.

This time when C.J. looked up he was grinning. "You already have," he answered wryly. Then pitching his voice so it would carry clearly to the gang of kids watching along the wharf, he said, "My shift will be over in about another twenty minutes. I'll be home right after that, okay?"

To Lion's relief, Bobbi didn't argue. Instead she nodded, turned, gave the two scowling older teens another sunny smile as she moved past them, and started back the way she had come.

Again prickles of uneasiness started chasing themselves across Lion's back. He had the feeling that the wharf had doubled in length since Bobbi first walked out on it. Now with each step she took he expected somebody to jump her from behind, for every pair of eyes was on her. What if somebody wanted to save face and prove who was smartest and strongest.

Fortunately, nobody did. Bobbi was off the wharf and back on solid ground.

"What the heck did you think you were doing?" Lion stormed, hoping the anger would keep her from guessing how scared he'd been.

She wasn't fooled. "Thanks for coming out as back up," she told him quietly, her eyes warm and grateful. "You didn't look as if you were the least bit scared, but I sure was."

Lion's anger was forgotten. "Looks can lie," he admitted with a grin. "Come on, let's get out of here."

For a second Bobbi paused and glanced back toward the wharf. "D'you think C.J. will be okay?"

"For the moment — now that you've made it clear that he's expected home in about twenty more minutes. But I'm not sure how long you'll be okay if we stick around much longer. In about two more minutes those big goons may decide to do a little face saving." As he spoke he moved off.

To his relief Bobbi followed. But she seemed strangely silent, and her face was creased in a frown. At last, in a carefully emotionless voice she said, "When we first came up the other kids were giving C.J. a bad time. D'you figure those things they were saying were just made up?"

"I dunno." Lion kept his own voice equally emotionless. "Maybe when C.J. gets home we should ask him."

However, long before C.J. got home Lion had forgotten all about asking questions. For when Bobbi stopped at the pasture to give the horses their suppertime oats and Lion went on alone to the house, he found Dad with his arms around Mrs. Hamilton.

He froze in the doorway. All his fears resurfaced. True, Dad wasn't kissing Mrs. Hamilton — just sort of comforting her. But still, he had his arms around her. What about Mr. Rutner and all that handyman fixing? Didn't Mrs. Hamilton realize that Mr. Rutner would make a much better second husband than Dad?

Chapter 14

Slipping back out of the doorway without being noticed, Lion headed outside. He intended to find an excuse to stay outside till supper time. Because he knew if he went in and bumped into either Dad or Mrs. Hamilton — or worse, both of them together — sure as anything his embarrassment would show. Better to wait till Bobbi was back from the pasture and C.J. was home from work. At least then there'd be somebody else to help carry the conversation.

But when suppertime came he discovered that it was just Dad, Bobbi and himself.

"Where are C.J. and his mom?" Bobbi asked in surprise as they sat down.

"At the police station."

Lion had been carefully concentrating on his plate of lasagna, but at this he looked up sharply.

"Not because they're in trouble," Dad said with a smile. "I asked them to go. I set up this meeting because it's time C.J. helped his own cause by showing a little co-operation and answering some questions. So far he has refused to say anything."

"Helped his own cause?" Bobbi asked, her face worried.

"And the cause of the rest of the boys as well." Dad's tone was calm and reassuring. "I told you as we were driving up here that Mrs. Hamilton asked me to try to make some sense of this strange housebreaking tangle, and speak on behalf of the boys involved."

"Because they're students in her school?" Bobbi asked.

Dad nodded. "The trouble is each one of them tells a different story."

"You mean they're lying?"

"Not at all. I think each one is telling the truth about his particular experience, but in each case that experience was different, because it seems each one of them was off on his own."

"So what did you mean about C.J. helping his own cause? Is he in more trouble than the others?"

Dad helped himself to a roll and started to butter it. "I think he will be if he continues to refuse to answer questions," he said after a moment. "I've already entered a plea with the court that the boys should he charged with nothing more than mischief. As far as the other boys are concerned, I'm confident the court will agree. They are underage, seemingly victims of deliberate deception by adults, don't seem to have benefited in any way themselves from this whole business, and have openly answered all the questions that the police have put to them. But C.J., who is the one person in the whole group who seems to have some idea about what was going on, refuses to say anything. That's why I asked Virginia to take him down." He glanced at his watch. "I hope she's not having any problems."

At the note of concern that had come into his voice all Lion's fears rushed back. Again the picture flashed across his mind of Dad with his arms around Mrs Hamilton. Quickly he ducked his head and once again began concentrating fiercely on his lasagna.

The silence stretched out. It began to be uncomfortable. He had to say something soon, Lion knew, or Dad would ask what was bothering him, and then what would he say? So latching onto the only thing that came to mind he told Dad about the scene on the wharf that afternoon.

"The kids were really picking on C.J.," he finished, "but if he really had been telling on the other guys it's his own fault. You'd think a clever guy like that would realize that you can't run home and tell the principal everything that happens at school."

"Is that what the other kids were saying he did?" Dad's voice was non-committal.

"Not in so many words, but that's what they meant."

For a second a look came into Dad's eyes that Lion couldn't read, then he looked down and concentrated on rearranging the crumbs from his roll into a round castle on the tablecloth. "Perhaps before C.J. and his mom get home," he said quietly, "I should explain a little about the reason for that name calling you heard today. It happened one day last spring. As school let out in the afternoon a group of students started to pick on a little boy in thick glasses. When the others closed around him, instead of standing up to them the youngster sat down and started to cry, which of course just egged the bullies on. C.J. saw what was happening and went to the boy's assistance.

"A parent walking by the school saw the whole incident and who was involved, and phoned the school office. By that time all the children concerned had gone home, but first thing next morning Mrs. Hamilton summoned the kids down to the office, then sent word home to their parents about their behaviour.

"Of course they all assumed C.J. had told on them when his mom had come home for supper the night before. Instead of checking, they assumed he was guilty and closed ranks against him." Dad gave his crumb castle a minor adjustment. Then his face softened and he looked back at Lion. "Things aren't always easy for the principal's son."

"And you want to do that to me!" Lion said angrily.

98

Dad looked confused. "Pardon?"

Instead of answering, Lion made an excuse about not being very hungry and headed for his room. But his thoughts changed from worrying about Dad and Mrs. Hamilton to puzzling about C.J. If C.J. had the guts to stand up to the bullies taunting that little kid on the playground, why hadn't he had the guts to stand up to whoever had set him up in the house-breaking scam that Dad had talked about? Why hadn't he just told them "no way" and walked off?

All at once Lion was remembering a night last spring at the park. Somebody had taken a grocery cart home from the supermarket, then abandoned it in the park, and the kids decided to smash it.

"Come on you guys, that's dumb!" Lion had said.

Max and Helmut had turned on him. "You planning to run home and tell your old man?" they taunted.

He'd backed down.

Maybe he and C.J. had even more in common than he'd realized. As soon as C.J. got home tonight he was going to talk to him.

But C.J. didn't get home till almost dark, and when he did he went straight to his room and closed the door.

Speaking to him would have to wait till tomorrow.

Lion was just falling off to sleep when it occurred to him that he'd been so busy worrying about C.J. he'd forgotten to tell Dad about the gardener. That was something else he had to do tomorrow. Not that it was important — but still, he'd tell him if he remembered.

Chapter 15

Talking to C.J. was topmost in Lion's mind next morning, but when he joined Bobbi and Dad at the breakfast table C.J. was still sleeping.

"The hospital said they thought Jock would finally be allowed visitors today," Dad said as Lion sat down. "So I'm going round there now to see. I'd like you two to come with me so Jock can meet you."

Talking to C.J. could wait till later, Lion decided. But when they reached Jock's room in the hospital they found the "No Visitors" sign was still on the door.

Dad stopped in dismay.

"Why don't you just poke your head in and say hi?" Lion suggested, seeing Dad's disappointment. "Mr. McPherson probably wants to see you as much as you want to see him."

"I can't disregard a posted order for No Visitors," Dad replied. "But I'm going to go and ask some questions." He turned and moved back down the hall toward the nursing station.

Lion watched as Dad moved around the shoulder-high partition at the end of the corridor and began talking to the uniformed nurse sitting at the desk behind it. When he was sure Dad was preoccupied, he moved back across the hall to Jock's partly closed door and peeked in.

"Bobbi! Come here!" he whispered, for the figure on the bed had seen him at the door and was beckoning to him to come in.

Hesitantly Lion moved closer.

"Are you — Syd's boy?" the man on the bed asked in a breathy voice.

Lion nodded. "And this is my sister." He nodded toward Bobbi who had moved up beside him.

"I — thought you — might be. Come closer — I have a message." Jock's voice was slow, and though his blue eyes were wide open they had the distanced look of someone fairly heavily sedated.

"We'll come back when you're feeling better —" Bobbi began.

"No — please." Jock's voice seemed a little stronger. The blue eyes closed for a moment, then they reopened. "Tell your dad — I came too early. Tell him — to check the traps. He can see from my place — when it's safe. Tell him — not to be fooled by the smoke screen — to check them now — not to wait."

That must be why Dad had spent so long looking at the view, Lion realized, for Jock's note had talked about the view too. *You've no idea how interesting —*

"How dare you disregard a 'No Visitor' sign!" The nurse who a moment before had been talking to Dad at the nursing station burst into the room. She advanced on Lion and Bobbi. "Do you want to make that poor man even sicker? Get out of here this minute!"

Lion was about to apologize and try to explain, but Dad had followed the nurse along the corridor and was standing in the doorway. Lion had never seen him so angry.

In furious silence Dad led the way back to the car. Still without saying a word he drove back to Mrs. Hamilton's and stalked into the house.

"We should have given him Jock's message," Lion whispered to Bobbi as they followed Dad up the walk, "even though he was so mad at us. It could be important.

101

We shouldn't have waited."

"If we'd told him in the hospital it would have been okay," Bobbi whispered back, "but once we got in the car we had to wait. Have you forgotten about that bug?"

He had! Completely forgotten! "I wonder if it's still there." He turned back to where the car was parked. Moments later he caught up with her again. "It's not," he told her in a relieved voice.

But Bobbi looked worried. "I wonder if they've put it somewhere else."

"Like where?"

"In the living room, maybe, or in the room Dad's sleeping in. Later on this morning if everybody goes out we should check."

There was no time to say anything more, for at that moment Dad and Mrs. Hamilton reappeared on the front walk. Again Dad ignored both Bobbi and Lion and moved toward the car, but Mrs. Hamilton stopped. "Tell C.J. when he gets up that we're leaving you three young people on your own for most of the day. First your father is coming with me to a rather important pollution control meeting that is scheduled at City Hall. Then we have appointments to talk to the people whose houses were robbed."

"Yes, m'am," Bobbi replied.

Mrs. Hamilton paused, frowning. Then she must have decided to say more, for she went on, "Tell C.J. that I'm really upset about the way he's treating Mr. Carswell. Mr. Rutner tells me C.J. refuses to explain or apologize. If you get a chance will you ask C.J. for me if he will at least phone Mr. Carswell?"

Lion nodded. As Mrs. Hamilton joined Dad in the car and they drove away, he asked Bobbi, "Who's Mr. Carswell?"

"I haven't a clue." Bobbi started toward the house. "So shall we look for that bug?"

"Might as well." Lion agreed. But as they went inside he changed his mind, for he could hear C.J. moving about in his room. Hunting for the bug could wait, he decided. First he had to pass on Mrs. Hamilton's message, then try to have that talk with C.J. and see if maybe there was some way he could help.

Mind you, a guy two whole years older might not want his help, but he intended to see. However, he wouldn't push. Not when C.J. was fourteen. And he wouldn't just blurt out the message from C.J.'s mom, either. He'd slip it in when he had the chance after he got the conversation going.

He moved up to C.J.'s door. Should he knock? That might be a mistake, too, he decided. Better to wait till C.J. came out. So putting his hands in his pockets, he leaned back against the wall and prepared to wait all morning if necessary.

The wait was over sooner than he expected. Just a few moments after he took up his sentry post, C.J.'s door opened.

"Hi," Lion said brightly, straightening up and trying to make it look as if he'd just that minute come out of his own room. "Did your mom tell you that yesterday when you were at work Mr. Rutner fixed that light socket in your room? He said you'd asked him to look at it."

"What light socket?" C.J. replied in a puzzled voice.

As a jump-start for conversation that hadn't exactly scored a ten. So instead he passed along Mrs. Hamilton's message about Mr. Carswell.

"But I've been to his house," C.J. said in a puzzled tone. Then his expression hardened. "As usual, Rutner thinks he knows everything and ends up just making trouble. I went to talk to Mr. Carswell right off." He started to push past Lion and move away.

That had been no good as a conversation starter either. It was now or never, Lion realized, so plunging right in he said awkwardly, "I was thinking that maybe we should talk."

C.J. stopped walking. He glanced back, looking self-conscious. "If it's about those kids down on the dock yesterday, pay no attention — "

"No," Lion interrupted taking a deep breath and swallowing his nervousness. "It's about how tough it is being a famous lawyer's kid — sometimes having to go along with things I don't really want to go along with — and having guys say I'm going to run home and squeal on them every time they think up some harmless scam. I thought maybe you'd have some advice."

The expression in C.J.'s eyes changed. The corners of his mouth pulled into a grin. "Welcome to the club. Incidentally, that was really decent of your sister to come to my rescue yesterday on the wharf."

Lion nodded. "Dad told us what really happened."

"Does she do things like that for you, too?"

Lion grinned. "Constantly,"

"You're lucky," C.J. said in a funny voice.

It was Lion's turn to be embarrassed. "So, d'you want to do something?"

For a moment C.J. didn't answer. Lion was about to say, "Forget it," and find something else to do with his day when again the corners of C.J.'s mouth lifted. "Something like what? Swapping stories about having a principal or a criminal lawyer for a parent?"

Lion hadn't realized that he'd been holding his breath. He let it out in a long relieved sigh. "Yeah." He grinned. "And how tough it is to keep any friends, because they figure at the first sign of pressure you'll turn tattletale."

"So to impress them and show just how un-chicken you are, you fall for a con that any six-year-old should be able to see through." C.J.'s voice had turned bitter.

"Like that housebreaking scam?" Lion asked quietly, knowing that the preamble was over.

For a moment C.J. studied him without answering. Then he took a couple of steps backward, nodded to Lion to come into his room, then closed the door behind him. "Actually it was pretty cleverly set up," he admitted, sitting down on the bed.

Lion slid his back down the closed door till he was sitting on the rug. "Ingenious clever, to quote my Dad."

"Your dad was right. It swung on five basic necessities — first, that the guys were eager enough to get the few summer jobs that they'd go along with having to prove they were gutsy to get them. Second, that the house to be used had either a pet door, or a bathroom transom window that was usually left partly open. Third, that the first guy in was small enough to squeeze through a pet door, or wriggle through a transom window."

"That's how you got in without damaging any locks or windows! Dad told us that was something that really baffled the police."

"Yeah, that's how I got in." There was no trace of pride in C.J.'s voice He sounded disgusted with himself. He half turned away, as if his confidences were over.

"You said there were five basics," Lion prodded. "That's only three."

C.J.'s attention came back. "Basic necessity number four was that the first guy in was good with dogs, and number five was that he was a chump." His voice had turned bitter again.

"And the first guy in was you." It was a statement not a question.

C.J. nodded. "I was the prize chump of all time. I should have suspected something when the boss guys said the kids were to leave the front doors of their houses open all the time they were inside."

Lion scowled. "Why?"

"They said it was so they could come around and check if they wanted to, and make sure the kids were following orders."

For a long time after that, neither boy spoke.

Then Lion pulled his knees up toward his chest, settled more comfortably against the closed door and in a matter-of-fact tone said, "Let's go back to numbers two and three. I'll give you a pet door, but nobody except a midget could wriggle through a transom. They're made so they only open about half way."

"Half way is enough if you're thin and supple."

For the first time it occurred to Lion just how thin and supple C.J. was. Ever since they'd arrived, C.J. had been wearing baggy sweat pants and a loose fitting t-shirt. But underneath, though he was fairly tall, he was small-boned and agile. "Gymnastics?"

"Five years."

So, maybe C.J. could get through a pet door or a transom window, Lion admitted silently. "But why did you agree to do it?"

"I told you I was a chump. I wanted to show the kids I wasn't a chicken or a Momma's boy, and I figured this was my chance." His voice turned sullen and his face tightened. "Besides, I trusted the guys who set me up. They said that baiting and dumping prawn traps could be really dangerous, so they had to make sure the guys they hired could be depended on in case things went wrong in that deep water."

Lion didn't find that hard to believe after what had almost happened to Jock.

"They said this test would show them which guys were the gutsiest, and I believed them."

Lion was still confused. "You wanna start at the beginning?"

For a moment C.J.'s rigid expression relaxed into a smile. "Sorry. I forgot you're a city guy and not a local." He resettled himself more comfortably on the bed. "Every summer a lot of kids get hired to bait and empty prawn traps. It's good money. But they only hire a certain number, and the people they do hire have to be good swimmers, good divers and have the guts to go down in really deep water if the cables get tangled or broken, or if something goes wrong.

"Of course, the minute I turned up to apply for a job," C.J. went on, "the rest of the kids started jeering, figuring I was the last guy with the guts for that job, and I probably would have left right then except at that moment two older guys came up."

"The same two guys who were crowding Bobbi on the wharf yesterday afternoon?"

"No. Much older. The two yesterday are just punky jocks hired to supervise the rest of us. They just give orders and push their weight around. The two guys who were there that first morning were probably twenty-five — maybe older. They knew my name, and came over and told me that they were glad I'd come to try out for a job, and that I could start working right away. But that when my turn came up I'd have to take the test like everybody else." C.J. scuffed the heel of one runner into the thick pile of the carpet. "I figured this was the chance I'd waited for to show the other guys I was just as gutsy as they were."

Lion didn't have to have that decision explained. He'd

have done exactly the same thing. "When you finally got to take your test, what did it involve?"

"A game of 'chicken'."

"A game of what?"

Again C.J. grinned. "That's what I thought when they first explained it." Again the amusement turned bitter. "By the time I discovered what was really going on it was too late."

For a minute, something on the sole of C.J.'s runner seemed to demand his attention. Then, still concentrating on his shoe, he continued, "The game was sort of like standing on the railroad track while a freight train is coming. Only we were in somebody else's house, and instead of a train barreling toward us it was the owners returning from work." His voice had turned hard and cold.

Lion was confused. "Everybody was in the same house?"

"No. Everybody was in a different one."

That must have been why Dad had said everybody's story was different, Lion realized. "So were they all gymnastics types who could get in through pet doors or transoms?"

"No. I went in first through the pet door or transom and opened the front door for them."

At last Lion understood. "But what about the pets that went with the pet doors? What dog worth his dog food is gonna let a complete stranger break into his master's house?"

C.J. grinned. "I told you basic necessity number four was that the first guy in had to be good with dogs."

"If you expect me to believe that after one word from you everybody's dog would lie down and play dead — "

"They don't." C.J.'s grin broadened. "But after one look at the nice juicy bone I was carrying they'd lie down and start eating."

It was Lion's turn to grin.

"If the dog was in the back yard," C.J. went on, "I was to give him the bone. As soon as he started eating, I was to race for the pet door, slide through and lock it behind me. If the dog was in the house, I was to stick my head in the pet door and call him. When he came out growling and bristling, I was to shove the bone at him, then try to make it back to the pet door first." C.J.'s face relaxed into a grin. "Some of the dogs made it clear that, bone or no bone, it'd be a mistake to hang around. When that happened I crossed that house off the list and went on to the next."

At the thought of C.J. being chased across somebody's yard by an angry doberman with a huge bone in his mouth, it was all Lion could do not to laugh. But he was afraid that might stop any more confidences, so he changed the laugh to a cough and said instead, "So, then what?"

"Once I was inside it was easy. I just locked the pet door so the guardian of the house couldn't decide he should come back in and take over his duties, then unlocked the front door for the guy who was waiting outside. He stayed to take his test and I went on to the next house on the list."

C.J. brushed the back of one hand nervously across his mouth. "The two older guys insisted that nothing was to be touched — no damage was to be done. All each guy had to do was go through to the living room, turn on the TV, and sit in front of it till he heard the family coming home. The longer he stayed after the owners first started up the walk, the more guts he had and the higher he rated on the hiring scale."

"Dad said something about leaving the TV on and a thank you note. What was that all about?"

"To prove we'd really stayed. The boss guys said that they *might* come around to check on us, but that they probably wouldn't. In which case, they'd have no real proof that we'd really gone inside because nothing was to be touched or damaged. They said anything as zany as leaving on the TV and writing a thank-you note was sure to be talked about … and they'd hear about it." C.J.'s attention switched back to the heel of his runner. "But I've been wondering if the real reason for the note was to incriminate people, so if things went wrong there'd be fall-guys. After all, handwriting can be identified …" C.J.'s voice trailed off.

"So each guy stayed till he heard somebody coming home, and then got out of there. Right?" Lion prompted.

"After he'd locked the pet door again, and at the last minute relocked the front door," C.J. agreed. "That was something the organizers made a big thing about. Everything had to be exactly the way it was when the owners left. So nobody would catch on to how I had let them in, because if anybody caught on it would spoil it for the guys who hadn't taken their tests yet."

"Not everybody took their test the same day?"

C.J. shook his head. "The first day two guys were tested. Next time, a couple more. Then on the third day we did five. At that point things blew up."

"How d'you mean blew up?"

For a moment C.J. didn't answer. Then he said in a bitter voice, "Because on the day we were doing five houses the boss guys changed the rules. They switched from 'don't touch or damage anything' to 'sit in front of the TV while we help ourselves to everything that's valuable.'"

At last, Lion understood. "And they'd covered themselves by saying they might come to check, so the boys weren't to worry if they heard anything."

C.J. nodded. "That morning I got a long distance phone call," he went on, sounding guilty now as well as bitter, "from some top boss I'd never spoken to before. He said he was calling from Vancouver. That I was to have my test that morning, and so were four other guys. He gave me the addresses of the five houses I was to open."

"Didn't that seem like an awful lot?"

"Yeah." C.J.'s voice was carefully non-committal, and he continued to avoid Lion's eyes. "But I hardly noticed because I was too busy worrying about something else."

"Something else like what?"

"Like discovering that the house I was to use for my own test belonged to Mr. Carswell. I was trying to think of a way to tell the man on the phone that I wasn't opening Mr. Carswell's house for anybody, when he launched into a big spiel about how glad he was I'd joined them because there wasn't anyone else he could depend on." A hard edge crept into C.J.'s voice. "After that I was feeling so smug and puffed up I convinced myself that since I was the guy going into Mr. Carswell's house there was nothing to worry about, because I'd been in there lots of times, and I'd make sure nothing was touched or damaged." The words trailed off for a moment. Then C.J. went on in a voice that rang with guilt and self-loathing, "Instead, while I was sitting blind and deaf memorizing what was happening on TV so I could fill in my report, a bunch of other guys quietly helped themselves to everything in Mr. Carswell's house that was valuable."

"Who was it who phoned?"

The self-disgust in C.J.'s eyes deepened. "You'd think I'd have had the sense to ask, wouldn't you, but I didn't."

"He probably wouldn't have told you even if you had," Lion told him.

A brief smile of thanks crossed C.J.'s face.

"While they were cleaning out the house, did you hear anything?"

"Not over the TV. Obviously that was the reason for making us listen and keep a record of what was on."

"Were the other four houses burgled too?"

C.J. nodded. "And because I'd been the one to let the other guys in, they all assumed I was in on the scam." A funny note came into his voice. "They told that to the police, and to the owners of all the burgled houses."

"Including Mr. Carswell?"

C.J. nodded.

Lion had caught the pain in C.J.'s voice. He wanted to ask why Mr. Carswell was so important, but he was afraid that might put an end to C.J.'s confidences. So instead he asked, "Why weren't the houses burgled on the first two days?"

"They were dry runs to sucker me in. The scam was strictly a once-only five-house deal with me set up as fall-guy." Again C.J. fell silent.

Risking the question he'd avoided asking earlier, Lion asked carefully, "Why is Mr. Carswell so important?"

C.J. was silent for so long, Lion thought he wasn't going to answer. When he finally looked up his face was tight. "He's my soccer and gymnastics coach. Since my dad died he's — "

"Your dad died?" Lion said in dismay.

"Of cancer. Last winter." C.J.'s voice was husky and tight and he was no longer looking at Lion.

Lion felt a rush of sympathy. That was rough. He thought C.J.'s dad had just taken off for a while, like Mom.

"We always did a lot of stuff together," C.J. went on. His voice had suddenly grown hoarse and he coughed to clear it. "Mr. Carswell was a really close friend of Mom and Dad's, so right away he started coming by a couple of times a week and taking me rowing, and fishing, and to ball games and stuff. He's a really neat guy. "I've been hoping if my mom ever decides to — "

He broke off, then finished abruptly, "Now he thinks I deliberately played him for a sucker and am sitting home laughing about it."

"Did he tell you that?"

"He didn't need to. Rutner told me."

"You said yourself that Rutner thinks he knows everything."

Again C.J. was silent.

"Is it because of the way Rutner butters up your mom that you don't like him?"

"Partly. Also, he's up to something, only I can't figure out what. But who cares about Rutner? What matters is finding a way to prove to Mr. Carswell that I didn't play him for a sucker. Only I haven't a clue even where to start."

"Sure you do. With those two guys who recruited you. They'll know the men who were behind it."

"Maybe, but it won't do me any good because both of them quit. They don't work around the dock any more."

"You could still talk to them."

C.J. grinned. "Don't I wish. One of them moved away, and the other guy high tails it every time I try to get near enough to talk to him."

With sudden intuition Lion asked, "Is he a tall muscular guy who wears a jean jacket? Was he outside your house that first afternoon when we drove up?"

C.J. nodded. "He was around again yesterday at the pasture. But every time I spot him and try to get close enough to talk, he sees me coming and takes off."

Talk about misunderstanding, Lion berated himself silently. Here he'd thought C.J. and the van driver were

113

friends! "Why d'you figure both he and the other guy quit the job at the wharf?"

"Maybe they didn't like diving down in 350 feet of water to check the traps — particularly not any of the traps near the octopus beds."

That thought was so appalling Lion felt sick.

In spite of his worry, C.J. laughed. "Octopus aren't that scary. That's a myth. They're shy, and playful and intelligent. Besides, the ones around here are just babies. This is a spawning area."

Lion tried to tell himself to believe it, but still he shivered. "They can't all be babies. Some of them have to be mothers."

C.J. grinned. "If you ever have to go down, just convince yourself that they're all good moms and are too busy with their babies to pay attention to you."

It was all very well for C.J. to joke, but Lion couldn't think of anything worse than diving down where there were octopus.

"But maybe the real reason they quit," C.J. went on, and there was no longer any trace of amusement in his voice, "was because they'd only been hired for one purpose."

"What do you mean?"

C.J.'s hands were clenched so tightly together in his lap that the knuckles showed white. "Maybe they were hired just to get me hooked and set up as fall-guy in that housebreaking scam so they could get at my mom."

"At your mom?"

"She's pretty active in the community. Her word carries a lot of weight. But it wouldn't if she were to get fired as principal."

"Fired?"

"Defeated in the election. It's gonna be held in a

couple of weeks." C.J.'s voice grew tight and self-conscious. "What better way to make sure she isn't re-elected than by nailing me as ringleader of a scam? Who's gonna elect her permanent principal in charge of 350 kids if she can't even bring up her own son properly?"

For a minute Lion was too stunned to reply, and before he could recover the jangling of the telephone interrupted.

With a look of relief C.J. got to his feet. "That'll be Mom remembering something she forgot to tell me to do." His affection for her sounded in his voice. "I'll be right back." But when he came back from the phone he was scowling.

"Was it your mom?"

"No. I've got to work another shift down at the wharf."

"But I thought this was to be your day off!"

"Me too. But Devon says he needs me. It's only for a few hours. That won't be bad."

The words were light but Lion caught the uneasiness behind them. Was it because C.J. knew the kids would be on his back again? "Why don't you quit when you hate it so much?"

"Because hanging around down there is the only way I'm gonna find out what is going on. Unless I can clear my name it could really ruin things for my mom."

Lion nodded. "So, maybe Bobbi and I will walk down later, and we can all do something when the shift is over."

C.J.'s face brightened. He checked his watch. "It's eleven-thirty now. Devon wants me there by twelve, but the shift is only four hours. Why don't you guys wander down around four. I'll be finished by then." He picked up his jacket and started toward the doorway.

"Aren't you taking your wet suit?" Lion asked.

"Devon said I wouldn't need it today."

"Is it okay if I tell my sister what you've just told me?" Lion asked, following C.J. toward the door. "Bobbi's really smart about things. Maybe if all three of us work on it we can come up with some answers."

"Don't I wish," C.J. tossed back over his shoulder, but it was clear from his tone that he didn't expect it to happen.

Chapter 16

Lion watched C.J. go, then went to find Bobbi. She was at the pasture looking after the horses. While she groomed Brie he repeated what C.J. had told him.

Even before he was finished, Bobbi was uneasy. "Let's not wait till four," she suggested. "We've got to exercise the horses and then feed them, but as soon as we're through, let's go straight down to the wharf." She broke off, then said in a thoughtful tone, "But maybe before we do we should take a few minutes and check to see whether or not that bug is still around someplace. If C.J. really is being set up to take the blame for everything, we can't take a chance on someone listening in to everything we say."

Bobbi was right, Lion decided. They'd intended to look for the bug a couple of hours ago as soon as they came home from the hospital. First they'd give the horses a run — there was lots of time for that — then they'd go back to the house to check for the bug. They could still be down to the wharf by four o'clock when C.J.'s shift would be ending.

But when they finished with the horses and went back to the house, a careful search of the living room, kitchen, hallway, and even the room Dad was using, revealed no sign of any bug.

Lion relaxed. "Good, it's gone."

Bobbi wasn't convinced. Putting a cautionary finger to her lips so Lion wouldn't say anything that might be overheard, she retraced her steps down the hall to C.J.'s room. Pushing the door open quietly she checked the window, under the bed and behind the door. Then she looked inside the closet.

She seemed to be taking such a long time that Lion was just moving over to see why, when she turned back and held up a torn piece of heavy black plastic.

"What's that?" Lion asked.

Again Bobbi put a finger to her lips. Moving closer she whispered, "Probably nothing, but why would C.J. hide it away in the back of his closet?"

"Who knows," Lion whispered back. "But we're looking for the bug, remember?"

Bobbi nodded. She put the piece of thick plastic back where she'd found it and continued her search. First she looked behind the drapes. Then she checked behind each of the posters on C.J.'s wall. Finally she moved over to the dresser. Pulling it out from the wall a few inches she looked behind it. For a moment she stood absolutely still, then she turned back to Lion and pointed. On the wall directly behind where the dresser had been standing was the same bug that had been in Dad's car all the way from the ferry.

All Lion could think of as he followed his sister out of C.J.'s room in silence, was that everything C.J. had told him that morning would have gone over that bug. And C.J. had just accused the van driver of being involved in the whole housebreaking scam!

That must be why C.J. had been called in to work when he'd been supposed to have the day off. The people who had set him up had heard him tell Lion all about it!

As soon as they were safely out of the room and far enough down the hall to be well out of range of the bug, he told Bobbi what he was thinking.

"Let's go down to the wharf right now, even if it is a

bit early," Bobbi said already moving toward the door.

Lion nodded.

But when they reached the wharf, even though it was only twenty minutes to four, the whole place was deserted. There was no sign of any one working the prawn traps, and there was no sign anywhere of C.J.

Chapter 17

Lion sat beside Bobbi on the wharf, staring at the deserted scene in front of them, grinding the heel of his runner into a worn groove in the wood. "We'd better find C.J. soon," he told his sister in a tight voice. "The van driver's record for arranging 'accidents' is pretty impressive."

Bobbi scarcely heard. She was staring at the deserted wharf. "Why aren't any of the other kids working?"

"Pardon?"

"Prawns don't stop feeding just because it's the weekend."

His sister was right, Lion realized. The traps had to be emptied and rebaited every day, and it was at about this time in the afternoon that this was done. So where were the kids who regularly worked this shift?

"And where's the man who telephoned C.J.?" Bobbi went on. "Obviously the call came from someone C.J. usually heard from about work shifts, because he didn't question it." She looked up and down the length of the wharf. "Why isn't he somewhere around?"

Lion's glance followed his sister's. "I dunno."

"I'm scared, Lion," Bobbi said quietly, getting to her feet. "I think we should find Dad and tell him."

Lion didn't need to be urged. This was no time to have dreams of solving this case themselves. Things had gone too far.

But though it was almost five o'clock when he and Bobbi arrived back at the house, Dad and Mrs. Hamilton still hadn't returned.

"Look! There's a message!" Lion pointed toward the

flashing red signal on the answering machine. "I bet it's from Dad saying where we can reach him."

"Or from C.J." Bobbi said hopefully. Already she was moving toward the machine. She pressed the play button.

Dad's voice greeted them. To Lion's relief Dad no longer sounded angry. "We're going to be longer than we thought talking to all the homeowners," the message began. "There's not much chance we'll be getting home till eight or nine this evening. So you three go ahead with dinner. Order in something." A smile came into his voice. "I'll reimburse you when I get home, so try to restrict yourselves to only a three or four course banquet." The message clicked off.

Lion stared at Bobbi in silence. He hadn't realized till that moment how much he'd been counting on Dad taking over. "So, I guess we just sit and wait."

"We can't! Not if Dad's not going to be home till eight or nine! We've got to try to find C.J. on our own. But first I'll leave a message for Dad in case he might come back early." She sat down at the desk and started writing.

Lion camped on the arm of the chesterfield and watched impatiently. "Come on, Bobbi!" he said at last. "You don't have to write a book — "

"Shhh. I'm almost finished. But I have to explain everything or he won't understand." For another few moments she continued writing, then she sat back. "There. Now we'll leave this where he'll see it as soon as he comes in." She looked around, then moved to the table and propped her note up on it. "Okay, if we have to find C.J. on our own, we'll just have to. Where should we start?"

Lion continued to camp on the chesterfield arm. "That's just it. We haven't got the foggiest idea where to start."

"Think of someone we can go to for help."

"The only person I've met on this whole trip, apart from C.J. and his mom, is the van driver." Lion's voice was sarcastic. "I'd just as soon not ask him for anything."

"There's that lady whose groceries you carried, but I guess we can hardly ask her to help when she has two small kids to look after."

Lion gave Bobbi a look. "She'd probably think it was a con and call the cops if two kids she didn't even know arrived at her door and asked her to come out and help look for some teenager who'd disappeared."

"You're right," Bobbi admitted with a grin. "So keep thinking."

For a long moment there was silence, then Lion said slowly, "I know C.J. doesn't like Mr. Rutner all that much, but he might help."

"Of course he would!" Bobbi's face brightened. "He seemed really nice when he came over that first night. The reason C.J. doesn't like him is probably because Mr. Rutner seems to really like Mrs. Hamilton."

"And I think he hopes Mrs. Hamilton will soon start to like him," Lion returned with a grin. "He was here most of yesterday playing Mr. Fix-it at Mrs. Hamilton's direction, and trying to make himself Mr. Necessary."

"All the more reason for us to ask him to help." Already Bobbi was looking in the telephone directory to find his number.

But after four rings the answering machine took over. No one was home at Mr. Rutner's house.

Again, Bobbi left a message, but this time a carefully worded one since she had no idea who might listen to it. She just told Mr. Rutner that Dad and Mrs. Hamilton were tied up on business till late this evening, which was why she and Lion were phoning him, because they were trying to locate C.J. She asked if Mr. Rutner had seen him anywhere, or knew where he was. If he did, when he got a chance, would he please get in touch with them or leave a message on their answering machine.

"Now what?" Lion said in a flat, defeated tone.

Bobbi didn't answer right away. "There has to be someone who'll help us," she said at last.

"Dad's friend Jock would, if they'd let us see him, but even if he's finally being allowed visitors they wouldn't let us in. Not after we broke the rules the last time."

"Keep thinking. Is there anybody at all who Dad talked about?"

Lion shook his head. "Except for the guy he said he was gonna hire to look after Jock's place — "

"Lion, that's it!" Bobbi exclaimed sitting up straighter. "The gardener who Dad hired! Remember, we saw him working out front! All we've got to do is tell him we're Dad's kids and he's sure to say he'll help."

"He'd be a nut if he didn't," Lion agreed wryly. "It's not going to take him long to realize that if he's already getting paid to look after Dad's friend, he can earn a nice extra bonus if he also looks after Dad's kids."

"Never mind what his reasoning is. The important thing is that if Dad hired him, he'll know we're not pulling a con when we ask him to help."

"Unlike that lady with the groceries," Lion said with a grin.

Bobbi didn't let on she heard. "Let's hope he hasn't finished for the day and gone home." She moved toward the door.

"Wait, Bobbi! Let's phone! It's miles to his place."

"What good will phoning do if he's out in the yard? Besides, it's not that far. Not if we take the horses."

She opened the door and headed out.

Lion stopped arguing and concentrated on catching

up. Actually, his sister was right. If they expected the gardener to help it was better to talk to him in person. And it wasn't that far. It shouldn't take more than fifteen or twenty minutes.

They spent that fifteen or twenty minutes debating unsuccessfully about the best way to announce to a complete stranger that their friend had disappeared and that they needed help to find him.

They hadn't reached a conclusion when Jock's house came into view.

Immediately, Lion pulled Raj to a stand, though they were still a good hundred metres away. He pointed to a shady clump of trees out of sight of the house. "Maybe we should leave the horses there," he suggested.

Bobbi didn't even try to hide her smile. "So we can make a quick getaway if we need to?"

"No way!" Lion blustered. "It's just that they'll be cooler there." Then for back-up he added, "We're sure not going to be welcome if we park two horses on that." He nodded toward the freshly cut lawn and spotless flower beds.

Bobbi continued to smirk.

"Okay, okay," Lion admitted at last, a sheepish smile creeping over his face. "Maybe I was thinking about a quick exit. But you've got to admit it was useful having the horses out of sight that last time up in Wells,"

Bobbi relented. "Actually, you're right."

They tied the horses where they'd be hidden from the house, then moved toward the brown and yellow building.

Lion started to sweat just the way he did whenever he got sent down to the office. Maybe Bobbi thought it was perfectly normal to walk up to some stranger and ask for help, but he sure didn't.

There was no sign of the gardener, but the hoses were going and the lawnmower hadn't yet been put away. "He must be inside," Lion suggested.

The gardener couldn't have seen them approaching, for he looked startled and uneasy when he opened the door to Bobbi's knock. For a second something crossed his face that made Lion think he recognized them. It was weird, because for a second Lion thought the gardener looked familiar too. But then he realized it was impossible. How could either of them recognize each other when they'd never met? Besides, if the gardener had recognized them and realized they were Dad's kids, he wouldn't be trying to close the door again as he was doing.

"Please wait," Bobbi begged, moving closer. "You don't know us, but we know who you are because it was our dad who arranged for you to come to look after Mr. McPherson's house."

The door stopped moving. Through the small opening that remained Lion could see the gardener's face. He looked thoroughly confused. Obviously not a mental heavy-weight, Lion decided, and he glanced over at Bobbi to see if she was thinking the same thing, but Bobbi didn't even glance his way.

"We need to talk to you," she rushed on in the same worried voice. "Please. We need to ask your help. I know it's almost suppertime, but could we come in for a minute?"

The gardener looked more uncomfortable than ever. He cast a quick look back over his shoulder which was so guilt filled that Lion began to wonder if he was harbouring a room full of illegal pot plants. But the next minute he'd recovered. The worried look faded. He actually smiled. To Lion's surprise, he stepped backward, held the door wide and invited them inside.

"Thank you," Bobbi told him, her relief sounding in her voice.

"We're looking for a friend of ours," she began as soon as they were inside. Then it must have occurred to her that she couldn't just blurt out to a total stranger that they were afraid their friend might have been kidnapped, for she broke off in confusion.

The gardener waited.

"We were thinking —" she began again in the same self-conscious voice, "— at least — we were wondering —" Again the words dried up.

Lion was unsuccessfully trying to think of some way to come to her rescue when from out of nowhere inspiration must have struck, for Bobbi relaxed. "We thought because you've got such a great view of the wharf and everything," she said brightly, taking a few steps closer to the picture window which overlooked both the ocean and the highway that hugged the shoreline, "that if our friend was anywhere around you might have seen him."

Lion sent his sister a private smile of approval. She deserved full marks.

The gardener continued to watch her warily. "I haven't seen anyone in the last little while." His voice was carefully casual. "What does this friend of yours look like?"

Bobbi described C.J.

"You say you are worried about him?"

Bobbi nodded.

"Because he was called in to work on the prawn traps down at the wharf, only he isn't there," Lion supplied, thinking it was time he provided some help.

The wary look in the gardener's eyes gave way to a smile. "If that's all that's worrying you, relax. Close to a dozen kids were on the wharf most of the afternoon, dumping and rebaiting prawn traps. But a squall seemed to be threatening to blow up." He nodded to the sky out over the ocean where threatening black clouds were still visible. "So the man in charge sent everyone home a little early." His smile broadened. "Instead of going straight home your friend has probably gone off with the other boys for a while to enjoy his unexpected free time."

It was such a logical explanation that Bobbi was embarrassed. "We should have thought of that ourselves instead of getting all worried," she said self-consciously. "We're sorry to have bothered you."

"No bother."

Bobbi turned back toward the door.

But Lion had noticed a weird-looking chart on the wall beside the picture window. Now that there was no longer any need to worry about C.J., he was curious. "What's that?" He moved closer.

"A chart of the ocean floor in this area," the gardener replied, moving over beside him. "Do you know anything about prawn fishing?"

Lion shook his head.

"Anybody who is licensed as a prawn fisherman can put down traps in the various feeding areas, but as a rule each fisherman tends to put all his traps in one general area. It makes it so much easier for dumping and rebaiting them. This map shows where the traps are."

"How do people know whose traps are whose?"

"By an identification tag."

Lion remembered what Dad had said about the traps sometimes being three or four hundred feet down. "Wouldn't a guy get pretty sick of swimming around on the ocean floor to check identification tags so he'd know which traps were his?"

The gardener laughed. "Very. But you don't have to

go down to check them. Every trap is attached to an orange marker buoy that floats on the surface of the water. The orange markers carry the same I.D. as the traps."

Lion was staring at the chart. It was marked top, bottom, and along both sides in distances and depths. Set against the distance and depth markings were dark black squares.

"Are those prawn traps?"

The gardener nodded. "And those are their I.D. numbers." He pointed to red pencilled figures beside each black square.

"What are those?" Lion asked, staring at several yellow shaded areas that had been drawn on the chart beside some of the prawn traps.

"Octopus spawning beds."

Lion's stomach turned. He swallowed hard. Was he ever glad he didn't have a job like C.J.'s. No matter how much he was offered, there was no way he'd go down anywhere near those prawn traps.

Bobbi had moved up beside Lion as the gardener had been talking. "Do any of those traps belong to Mr. McPherson?" she asked.

For some reason the gardener seemed amused. "Yes." He glanced toward the picture window. "You can't see them from shore level because of the curve of the shoreline, but we're high enough that you can see them from here." He pointed to a semi-circle of orange marker floats in the far distance. "Jock has quite a lot down. You can see them marked on the chart here." He nodded toward a dozen or more traps in a group, all sitting higher on the graph than the others. Where most of the black squares sat at levels of 300 feet or deeper, these were all only 50 or 60 feet down.

"How come they aren't very deep?" Bobbi asked.

"That particular area is fairly shallow," the gardener explained, "but it's filled with rocky crevasses, and so is an excellent area for prawns."

Lion wasn't even listening. He was staring in horror at the yellow shading that had been sketched in all around Jock's traps.

The gardener guessed what he was thinking and laughed. "You're right. Rocky crevasses are not just favourite areas for prawns. They're also favourite spawning areas for octopus." His grin widened. "Actually, Mr. McPherson took a lot of teasing when he decided to put his traps in that area this season. No one else wanted to go anywhere near, but he says he likes octopus and doesn't mind sharing his space."

Any interest Lion had in prawn fishing had evaporated long ago. Praying his stomach would behave, he turned back to the picture window and concentrated instead on the peaceful scene below — the waves rolling methodically toward the shoreline, the winding highway that edged the water, and a couple of empty fishing boats lazily bobbing at anchor.

The gardener moved to join him. "To be honest, I don't like octopus either," he said, still sounding amused. He nodded toward the view. "This is much more interesting. A person can stand here and gaze out and never get tired of it."

At that moment a van, travelling too fast, came around the corner onto the stretch of highway directly below. A small car had been driving slowly along the same stretch, obviously sightseeing. Too late the van saw it. Frantically the driver pulled out, and only barely managed to get by without sideswiping the smaller car.

"That just about happened to us," Lion said, watching the near accident.

Before he could go on and add that in their case he wasn't too sure it hadn't been intentional, the gardener said mildly, "There are some bad stretches of highway on this road. That's one of them right down there, but an even worse one is the stretch just after you leave the ferry that you're talking about." For a moment longer he stared at the view, then he turned back. "Here's something else you might be interested in," he said, leading Lion across the room to a chart on the opposite wall. "It's a tide chart. Right now we're having the highest evening tides of the whole summer."

"Is that good?" Lion asked.

"For fishing, yes. But I wouldn't advise you to go out swimming. At least not in the evening around nine or nine-thirty. For these next few nights the undertow at high tide will be so strong it will be almost impossible even for strong swimmers to stay afloat against it. This shows how the tides vary." And he pointed to the varying tide line that was marked against twenty-four-hour time markings.

Lion was still studying the tide chart and lining up his next question when Bobbi caught his arm.

"We should go," she said in a quick bright voice. "Remember, we promised C.J. we'd give him another riding lesson as soon as he got through work. He's probably back home by now wondering what's happened to us. If we don't show he'll be really disappointed."

Lion bent and pretended his running-shoe lace needed attention so his expression wouldn't show, for his sister knew as well as he did that C.J. had no intention of ever taking another riding lesson. Also, C.J. wouldn't worry in the slightest if they didn't show. Obviously Bobbi was giving him a signal of some kind, and until he knew what it was about he'd play along. His sister didn't give signals for no reason.

He waited while she thanked the gardener once again, then followed her out of the house and across the lawn, listening to her steady chatter about plans for the rest of the day. He made no attempt to interrupt as she continued to chatter all the way back to the clump of trees where the horses were tethered. Then, safely out of sight of the house, he caught her arm. "What's wrong? Why were you in such a hurry to leave?"

"Because the gardener is in on the scam," Bobbi replied in a low frightened voice. "For a minute I was afraid maybe he'd guessed I was suspicious and wasn't going to let us leave."

"But that's crazy! How can he be in on the scam?"

"I don't know, but he is. Otherwise he couldn't have known which stretch of highway we were on when we nearly had that accident."

She was right, Lion realized with a shock. And he hadn't even caught the gardener's slip!

"Also," Bobbi hurried on, "Dad couldn't have hired him."

"Why not?"

"There wasn't time. Think back. It was after Jock's accident when we swung by his house that Dad said he'd hire someone to look after it. But then we drove straight to Mrs. Hamilton's. Dad didn't do any phoning to arrange anything that night — we were all too busy talking to Mrs. Hamilton and Mr. Rutner. And he didn't do any phoning early next morning because we were all busy talking at breakfast. Then as soon as breakfast was over he and Mrs. Hamilton went to check on Jock and then they had an appointment at the police station. The earliest he could have started phoning to find someone to look after Jock's place would have been late morning, and the gardener was already at work by then."

Again his sister was right, Lion realized. The grass that had badly needed cutting when they had driven by with Dad that first night, had been freshly cut and trimmed when they had walked by on the way back from the wharf. The gardener must have been at work for an hour at least.

"We assumed Dad had arranged for the gardener because he said he was going to," Bobbi went on, "but we never actually spoke to him about it."

It was true. They'd been going to razz him about being swift off the mark, only they forgot. "But if Dad didn't hire him, then who — ?"

Lion realized what the answer was. *I'll arrange for someone to look after Jock's place*, Dad had said as they were driving. The van driver who was listening must have decided to hire a gardener before Dad had a chance to.

But why?

Lion told Bobbi what he was thinking.

For a moment, neither of them said anything.

Chapter 18

"The thing I can't understand," Bobbi said thoughtfully, shredding a long blade of grass from its stem, "is why all of a sudden they seem to be scared of C.J."

"Obviously they're afraid he'll start telling other people what happened, now that he's told me."

"But why weren't they afraid of that before? Those five houses were robbed a couple of weeks ago with C.J. set up as fall-guy. If they'd been worried about C.J. clearing his name, why didn't they do something about it before this?"

"Maybe because nothing has been said yet publicly," Lion replied. "Remember Dad said the police were keeping everything quiet because so far they had no evidence of any break and entry damage, and no evidence that the missing things had actually been stolen."

"You mean the stuff that disappeared might have been moved out secretly for some reason by the owners themselves?"

"Maybe. I suppose it's the sort of thing that the police have to consider."

"But the police must know that C.J. was the one who let everybody in. The kids must have all admitted that."

His sister had a point. "But without any evidence, what can they accuse him of?"

For a moment there was silence. Then Lion said thoughtfully, "Maybe the police are waiting and not saying anything because they're hoping that sooner or later somebody is going to lead them to the missing stuff."

"But that doesn't explain why all of a sudden today

somebody has decided that C.J. is too dangerous to leave walking around."

"No, it doesn't," Lion agreed. Then he stopped abruptly. "Yes it does!" he corrected himself excitedly. Bobbi looked up sharply.

"Remember Dad saying that the strange thing was that none of the stolen stuff had turned up anywhere?" Lion hurried on. "Dad said nothing has turned up in any pawn shops, or been caught by customs at the border, or been discovered being sent through the mail. Maybe the reason is that the stuff has been kept hidden all this time — hidden right close to where it was stolen — and the people behind the con are suspicious that C.J. may have discovered where it is!"

For a moment Bobbi didn't answer. Then in a tight, frightened voice she said, "If that's true, and if they've got C.J. hidden away someplace, they may decide he's too dangerous to let go — ever."

A needle of fear corkscrewed somewhere deep in Lion's middle. He was remembering what would have happened to Jock if that other fisherman hadn't jumped in quickly enough — and what would have happened to Bobbi, Dad and him on the highway if Dad hadn't been such a good driver. "When you get those feelings of yours about people being in danger," he said at last, "you sure don't fool around, do you?"

"Stop making jokes," Bobbi retorted. "We've got to find C.J., and since we've run out of people to ask for help, we've got to work things out for ourselves. So think." For the past few minutes they'd both been standing by the horses, ready to mount, but now Bobbi retied Brie to a branch and sat down on a grassy spot between the trees. "What do we know?"

"Practically nothing."

"Thanks a lot."

"All right," Lion agreed, sitting down on the grassy dirt beside her and starting construction on a trench with the heel of his running shoe. "We know C.J. was called in to work, and that he's disappeared. We also know that the person who called him in and who apparently ran the work crew has also disappeared."

"Not necessarily," Bobbi countered.

"Then if Devon hasn't disappeared, where is he? Why isn't he on the wharf?"

Instead of answering Bobbi stared at him in alarm. "Why didn't you tell me that sooner?"

"Tell you what?"

"That his name was Devon."

"What difference does it make?"

"Just the difference between C.J. being okay and C.J. not being okay." Bobbi's voice was acid. "In case you've forgotten, little brother, that was the name Dad used when he was telling us about Jock's partner."

Of course! Why hadn't he remembered? "Jock and his partner Devon head out to fish ... " Dad had said. Then a new thought struck. "That's who the gardener is! Why didn't I twig sooner! That's why he looked familiar when he first opened the door! We saw him on the shore that first afternoon when Jock almost drowned, but I was so busy looking at Jock I hardly noticed anyone else!"

"I didn't look at him at all," Bobbi admitted with regret.

Now Lion was really scared, for they'd seen Devon in action on the fishing boat, standing by doing nothing while Jock was being dragged overboard — then on the shore elbowing Dad out of the way.

"That explains why he's living inside Jock's house instead of staying outside as he should be if he really was

135

the gardener," Bobbi said thoughtfully. "It also explains how he knew so much about the fishing areas, and the prawn business." She paused, then added ruefully, "Actually, we should have guessed something was wrong when he lied about Jock."

"Lied?"

"When he was showing you that underwater chart he said Mr. McPherson didn't mind sharing his space with the octopus, but Jock would have minded. He said in that letter to Dad that he didn't like octopus. Devon's crack about his not minding sharing his space had to be a private joke."

Lion's frown deepened.

"Whatever is going on, Jock's house is somehow involved," Bobbi went on. "Over the bug they heard Dad saying he'd arrange for someone to look after Jock's place, and they didn't want to let an outsider in for fear he'd stumble onto whatever was going on. So they installed Devon as gardener before Dad had a chance to do anything."

Lion nodded, for it made sense. "So let's go back to what we know. First, C.J. was called in to work, only when we went down to meet him at the end of his shift, he'd disappeared."

Bobbi took over. "The person who called him in to work was Devon, who was his boss for the prawn fishing operation, and who was also Jock's fishing partner."

"And who is now pretending to be the gardener at Jock's house," Lion added. "What else do we know?"

"That when we first arrived at Jock's house Devon didn't want to let us in," Bobbi said.

Lion nodded. "I'll say he didn't. First he practically shut the door in your face, then he gave such a worried look over his shoulder I wondered if he had a pot growing operation in the living room."

Instead of smiling, Bobbi frowned. "Did he? I was so busy trying to think of something to say that wouldn't sound ridiculous that I wasn't really paying attention. What did he turn and look at?"

"I thought he just looked around the living room but I guess it could have been at anything."

"Are you sure he looked over his shoulder, not towards the door or down the hall?"

"It was over his shoulder."

"There must have been something back there he didn't want us to see," Bobbi said thoughtfully. "He must have glanced back to check."

"But there was nothing in the room but furniture and the usual stuff everybody has in their living room. Except for that chart on the wall, but he couldn't have been worried about us seeing that, or he wouldn't have gone to all that trouble explaining what it meant."

Bobbi scowled. "What would have been directly behind him?"

"Like I said, the living room furni — "

"The picture window!" Bobbi interrupted eagerly. "Directly over his shoulder would have been that picture window. So maybe he wasn't checking something in the house, but something *outside* — something he was afraid might be visible through that picture window! Think Lion. You were standing staring out the window for ages. What was there outside to see?"

"The highway and the ocean."

"What else? Try to remember."

Lion closed his eyes. "The highway, and the van nearly side-swiping that little car — and the waves coming in and breaking against the rocks on the shore — and farther out a couple of empty fishing boats bobbing at anchor — "

"Fishing boats?" Bobbi's voice was sharp. "Was one of them Jock's?"

"I didn't look that closely. In any case I probably couldn't have told even if I had looked closely. They all look pretty much the same."

"I bet anything one of them was," Bobbi said in a low excited voice. "Maybe that was what Devon turned to check — Jock's fishing boat."

Lion was lost. "So what if he did? Why is that important?"

"Because they could hide C.J. on that boat and no one would ever know." A sharp worried edge had come into Bobbi's tone. "C.J. wasn't in Jock's house — if he had been, Devon would never have let us in. He wasn't anywhere on the road between the wharf and Jock's house or we'd have seen him. What easier way to hide him away without anybody even noticing than by sending him out to the fishing boat on some cooked-up errand, then having somebody waiting out there to make sure he didn't come back."

Lion had to admit it made sense. The other kids on the wharf wouldn't think anything of it if Devon sent C.J. out to the boat. Then, while he was still out there, Devon could use the storm as an excuse and send everybody else home early. None of the other guys would hang around waiting for C.J. to come back — not when they all had it in for him because they thought he'd told tales on them to his mother.

"But why, when Devon was so unfriendly at first, did he suddenly get so friendly?" Lion asked.

"Maybe he wasn't sure whoever had been on the boat with C.J. was safely back on shore yet, and until he was sure, maybe he figured the safest thing was to keep us with our backs to the window studying his prawn chart."

"Or the tide chart," Lion agreed, remembering Devon's attempt to get them interested in that as well. "When we were looking at it we had our backs to the picture window too."

Bobbi nodded.

"Should we go out to Jock's boat and check?"

"How?" Bobbi asked dryly.

"Swim."

"With Devon keeping watch from that picture window? No wonder Dad called Jock's house a great look-out spot."

Bobbi was right of course. "So does that mean waiting till after dark?" Lion asked.

"Mmmm-hmmm. But look on the bright side. If we can't do anything without being seen, neither can they. Remember they don't know we're in this just by ourselves. They probably think we've passed along everything we know to Dad and Mrs. Hamilton."

That thought made Lion feel slightly better. Then a new thought struck. "It's okay for us to sit here and wait till dark, because we're not in any danger. But what if —" He coughed to clear the funny note that had come into his voice and said again, "What if C.J.'s hurt or in some kind of danger? What if he can't wait till dark."

"I've been thinking about that too," Bobbi admitted quietly. "But I think he'll be okay if we spend the time until then sitting sun bathing."

"Sun bathing!" Lion sounded incredulous. He glanced at the sky. "In another hour the sun's going to be down."

"Then we'll spend the time sitting sunset watching," Bobbi amended. "The thing is, I don't think they'll risk doing anything to C.J. if there are people on the end of the wharf staring out to sea, watching that boat."

At last Lion understood. He grinned and got to his feet. "Let's get started sunset watching."

Since a long wooden wharf was hardly the place for horses, they left them where they were tethered out of sight in the trees, and walked back down to the end of the wooden structure. As they came back into full view of the picture window Bobbi whispered, "Don't look around. Act innocent."

Lion felt as self-conscious as a fish in a glass aquarium tank being stared at by a whole classroom of kids — all armed with dart guns. Just how did his sister think he could act innocent and ignore the prickles running across his shoulders and down his arms? But at least he'd managed to resist the impulse to glance back and see if Devon was watching from that window. When they reached the end of the wharf he settled himself on the hard wood planking and stared out at the water, still resisting the temptation to look backward.

The silence stretched out.

He had a feeling it was going to be a long time before sunset.

At last he broke the silence. "Fishers are dumber than I thought." He was studying the water. "Whoever built this wharf either wanted to make work, or had a lot of lumber to get rid of."

"Pardon?"

"Look where it's sitting — about three quarters of it is on dry land. If they were going to build a wharf, you'd think they'd have built it so it was out in the water." He sounded unimpressed. "Or else only make it a quarter as long."

Bobbi tried not to smile. "I always suspected that class of yours was taking too much time off for field trips or getting too many in-service days. Or maybe you were down in the office those days."

"What days? What are you talking about?"

"The days your class was studying about tides." Bobbi's voice was amused.

"Oh. Tides," Lion attempted to recover, for he should have realized that himself, especially with all those diving lessons he'd taken over the past couple of years.

"The tide had just finished going out when we first went to Jock's house," Bobbi went on. "Now it's coming back in. If you look you'll see the water moving right now. By high tide the whole wharf will be in deep water almost up to the deck planking."

"What time will that be?"

"According to Dad it varies every day, like the sunrise and the sunset. I should have looked closer at that chart Devon wanted to show us."

"Hey, I remember!" Lion exclaimed. "Devon mentioned it when he was explaining that the evening tide right now is about the highest it gets all year. He said high tide tonight would be around nine or nine-thirty, and not to go swimming because when the tide is high the undertow can be really dangerous."

"I guess I was so busy wondering how I was going to get you out of there that I didn't listen," Bobbi admitted sheepishly.

Lion continued to stare at the water below them. It wasn't moving all that fast right now. He wondered if Devon was right about it coming with a real rush when the tide was full.

Not that he really cared, but it was a way to keep his mind busy and avoid looking back at that picture window.

Chapter 19

They continued to sit at the end of the wharf. No one came near them, and no one went near Jock's fishing boat.

At one point Lion suggested going back to the house to see if Dad might have come back.

"We can't," Bobbi told him firmly. "The minute they see us leave they'll move C.J. They must know we've worked out that C.J. is on that boat, otherwise why would we stay here? Besides, going home won't help, because Dad won't be back yet. He said it would be late this evening."

Lion lapsed back into silence.

Suddenly, Bobbi sat straighter.

Instantly Lion was alert. "What is it?"

"I've been thinking back about everything that's happened," Bobbi said slowly, excitement building in her voice, "and this idea keeps jumping out at me. It seems completely crazy, but it won't go away."

"What idea?"

"Where the stolen household stuff may be hidden."

"Where?" Lion asked eagerly.

"In Jock's prawn traps."

Lion let his breath out in a disgusted grunt. "Funny, funny. Come on, Bobbi, be serious."

"I am. Think back, Lion! That very first message of Jock's was about nothing but prawn fishing."

"Prawn fishing and octopus," Lion corrected with a grin, "and about eight arms being dangerous when divided by four."

"All right, prawn fishing and octopus," Bobbi agreed,

"but mainly prawn fishing. Jock's second message on the phone was again about prawn fishing. Then, when we managed to speak to him in the hospital and he urged us to take a message to Dad — it was for for him to go down and check the traps — not to be scared of the octopus and not to wait."

Lion wanted to point out that Jock had been so heavily sedated that he probably didn't even know what he was saying, but his sister looked so earnest and so worried that he replied instead, "So exactly what are you saying?"

"That somehow this whole thing is tied in to prawn fishing. It's prawn fishing that links Devon and Jock — it's prawn fishing that Jock keeps talking about in his messages to Dad — and it's prawn fishing that C.J. got invited to try out for."

"By the van driver and some other guy."

Bobbi nodded. "C.J. admitted that if it hadn't been for them he'd have left that first day and not bothered trying to get a job at all. Somebody wanted him to be part of the fishing team."

"That wasn't because of the fishing," Lion protested. "That was because the test for getting hired was that phoney chicken game, and they wanted him in that so they could set him up for the housebreaking."

"I know, but it's all connected! The housebreaking resulted in a nice cache of stolen goods which then had to be hidden away somewhere till it was safe to sell them or move them. And what better place than in Jock and Devon's prawn traps? It was the perfect hiding place because Jock never came up till late and so wouldn't know, and Devon was in on the scam!"

For a minute Lion looked almost convinced, then he raised his eyes skyward. "End of joke. You almost had me suckered in. There's no way those guys would go to the trouble of ripping off all those houses, then store the valuable loot under water in open mesh traps where it'd get absolutely ruined."

"It wouldn't if it was in waterproof bags."

"Pardon?"

"Jock's prawn traps could have been lined with waterproof liners — thick plastic liners," Bobbi added, slowing the words for emphasis and watching Lion closely. "Like that piece of torn plastic that we found in C.J.'s closet and wondered why he'd have saved it."

"You think he dove down to check, and brought up that piece of plastic for proof? D'you think they know he did, and that's why they decided all of a sudden to stop him from talking to anybody?"

Bobbi nodded.

"That would explain why he didn't want to stay in the pasture with us that first night, but was in such a big hurry to get back to the house," Lion agreed thoughtfully. "He said he had something to do. Obviously it was to get rid of that piece of plastic that he'd left under the lilac bush before the van driver saw it and realized he was on to them!"

Again Bobbi nodded. "No wonder he was so uptight and preoccupied."

"But if any prawn traps had been fitted with waterproof liners the other fishers would notice," Lion argued.

"Not when prawn fishers don't go down to check their traps. Remember what Dad said? The only time they go down is when there's trouble. The rest of the time they winch them up. And even if they did go down to check their own traps they wouldn't go snooping around Jock's when they're right in the middle of that octopus spawning ground."

Lion's stomach turned. At least about that his sister had a point. There was no way he'd go checking any traps in octopus spawning grounds — no matter how many millions of houses had been robbed.

A smile had come into Bobbi's eyes at Lion's reaction. Now it faded. "We've got to go down and see. We've got to do more than just rescue C.J. — we've also got to find out if that is where the stuff is hidden. Because if it is, that proves Devon was behind it, and that he was using C.J." She glanced at the sun, then back toward Jock's fishing boat. "We can't do anything about rescuing C.J. till dark, because Devon can see the fishing boat from Jock's picture window. The minute we make a move toward it he'll be after us. But if one of us sits here watching so they can't move C.J., the other one can use the time until dark checking out Jock's traps."

"Devon isn't going to sit back and do nothing while we check the traps for proof, any more than he's gonna sit back and do nothing while we head out and rescue C.J."

"But he won't know! He won't be watching the bay because he won't be expecting us to dive down in that water — particularly not after that big warning he gave us about how dangerous the night tides were. In any case, we've got to chance it. We'll just have to hope that Devon assumes that whichever one of us has gone, has gone back to Mrs. Hamilton's."

Lion was finding it hard to think about anything except that filmy shading of yellow around Jock's dozen prawn traps on the chart Devon had shown them. Even thinking about it made his stomach turn. Was that why Devon had shown it to them? To scare them? Well, if it was, he'd succeeded.

"All the experts say that octopus aren't scary," Bobbi said quietly.

C.J. had said that too, Lion remembered, but he hadn't believed C.J. And he wasn't going to believe Bobbi. There was no way he could go down and check those traps — no matter whose life was in danger. Seizing on the first excuse that came to mind, he blustered, "They couldn't be hiding the stolen household stuff in prawn traps. They aren't big enough. Remember Dad said they were only about two feet by one foot by one. What sort of household stuff could you store in something that size?"

"Lap tops, radios, microwaves, jewellery, china, silver, watches, CD's, video games — "

"Okay, okay," Lion interrupted since it was obvious his sister was prepared to go on indefinitely.

"You've done some deep water diving. Please, won't you go down?"

Lion had been avoiding her eyes, but now he looked up and met them squarely. "I can't Bobbi," he admitted honestly. "I'll swim out to the boat to check it, or I'll stay here and keep guard — I'll even go back to Jock's house and try to distract Devon's attention if that will help — but I can't go down into those octopus beds."

Bobbi's expression softened. She nodded. "Okay, then I will. But I'll need a wet suit."

"You could use C.J.'s — the one he had on yesterday afternoon. He didn't take it with him when he went to the wharf today." Lion paused, then added, "Maybe you'd better bring his oxygen tank too."

Instantly Bobbi looked worried. "I don't know how to use one."

"On second thought, you won't need it," Lion said quickly, afraid if he insisted on the tank he'd be the one who had to go down. "You don't need anything to go down just twenty feet or so."

Again Bobbi glanced at the sun. "I'll ride back to the

house for C.J.'s suit and be back well before dark. Make lots of noise while I'm gone so they'll know you're watching."

Lion nodded.

He was ashamed to discover how lonely he felt as he watched his sister disappear. He waited till she and Brie were out of sight then took one quick nervous glance around. Nobody was on the wharf, but that didn't prove anything. Devon — or the van driver — was probably watching him right this minute from that picture window.

He tried unsuccessfully to think about something else — anything else.

He glanced around. The sun was noticeably lower. He hoped Bobbi would hurry.

If he'd been ashamed at how uncomfortable he'd been when his sister left, he was even more ashamed at the wave of relief that swept over him as at last through the gathering shadows he saw her coming back into view. "So, have you got everything?" he called loudly to cover his feelings.

Bobbi threw him a furious look. Then when she was close enough she said in a disgusted undertone, "Why don't you just send them a telegram and tell them exactly what we're planning?"

"Sorry."

Ignoring Lion she moved toward the end of the dock. Pulling C.J.'s wet suit from the large plastic bag she'd carried it in, she put it on over her jeans and t-shirt. Then she tucked a knife she'd also brought back with her into the belt of the suit.

"Hey, good thinking," Lion applauded, nodding at the knife. If there really were waterproof liners in the prawn traps she'd need that knife to see what was inside.

Checking the suit one last time, Bobbi turned back to

147

Lion. "Think back to that chart on the wall that Devon showed us. How far do you figure Jock's traps were from here?"

"A hundred yards — not much farther."

"A hundred yards! In that frigid water!"

"That won't be bad in a wet suit."

"Then you do it."

Lion grinned. "With luck there'll be a waterproof compass in that suit. Look in there." He pointed to a large zippered pocket.

Sure enough the compass was inside, mounted on a wrist band.

"Put it on."

Bobbi did as she was told.

"The prawn traps that Devon showed us were all sitting in a sort of semi-circle just beyond that curve of shoreline." Lion pointed at a 45 degree angle from the end of the dock. "Set the compass to point out there and stick to that line. Once you can see around the curve you shouldn't have any trouble spotting the orange markers floating on the surface."

Bobbi nodded. Again she checked the sky. The sun had completely set and shadows were starting to darken over the water. Letting herself down into the gently moving waves she positioned the compass, gave Lion a tense smile, and set off.

This time the wait was even longer and more nerve wracking than when his sister had gone back for the diving suit. Maybe because it was dark, Lion decided. Just as he was sure something awful must have happened, he saw Bobbi's dark suited figure swimming back toward him.

"The traps are filled with plastic liners!" she told him in an excited whisper as soon as she reached the end of

148

the dock where he was waiting to pull her back out. "Heavy thick black plastic. I checked three traps and the same liners are in all of them."

"What about the octopus?" Lion asked, voicing the thought uppermost in his mind.

For the first time Bobbi grinned. "I wasn't exactly delighted to see them," she admitted, "but they didn't bite, or anything."

"Octopus don't bite," Lion retorted, suspecting that she was deliberately making fun of him.

"All right, then they didn't squeeze, or shoot dye at me, or do any of the things they always seem to do in Hollywood movies."

"So did you get some proof?" Lion said, eager to change the direction of the conversation. "Were you able to make a hole in one of the liners?" He nodded toward the knife in her belt.

Bobbi was starting to peel off the wet suit, but now she stopped and looked over at him. She shook her head. "I'm sorry, Lion. I kept trying, but I couldn't get the knife through the thick stiff plastic." She looked down. "Then I started to panic." Her voice was guilty and apologetic. "I needed to breathe and I didn't know how long it would take me to get back to the surface." She looked away then added in an even smaller and more embarrassed voice, "For a minute I thought I wasn't going to make it. When I finally did, I was too terrified to go back down and try again."

Lion nodded. Actually, for an inexperienced diver she'd done well to go down at all.

For a moment Bobbi watched him. Then in a voice that sounded more normal she said, "Won't you go down just for one quick trip? We've got to get some proof — "

"Bobbi, I can't!"

"The marker buoys are easy to spot," she went on as if he hadn't spoken. "They're exactly where you said they'd be." She pointed to the compass setting he'd given her. "It'll be easy for you because you've gone deeper than that lots of times. You know just how long it takes to go up and down, and you can hold your breath way longer than I can. All you've got to do is make a hole in one of those waterproof liners, then grab the first things you see that can be identified as belonging to one of those burgled houses."

All the time Bobbi had been swimming out to the prawn traps Lion had been feeling increasingly ashamed and guilty. It was true — he'd done lots of deep water diving while she'd done hardly any. But guilty or not, he couldn't go down where there were octopus. "It's not a question of locating the marker buoys or holding my breath," he defended himself gruffly. "It's what happens if I throw up when I'm twenty feet under water."

Bobbi was concentrating on taking off the wet suit. "Then don't throw up."

"Easy for you to say! I've already told you I feel like throwing up even thinking about those octopus."

At that she looked up and met his eyes. He could see the glistening of tears in hers. "So do I," she admitted simply.

All that teasing she'd done in the car had been covering the fact that she was as scared as he was!

A guy couldn't be a bigger sissy than his sister —

He held out his hand for the wet suit she'd taken off. "Thank you," she told him quietly.

Not quite sure where to look, Lion turned away. Then a new thought struck and he felt better. Bobbi had probably scared away any octopus near those prawn traps. If he hurried, he could be down and back before they returned.

He put on the suit, took the compass his sister was holding out, then tucked the knife in his belt as she had. Lowering himself into the water he started to swim. Bobbi was right about it being cold. It was freezing! For a minute he wondered why. After all, it was still the middle of the summer — then he remembered about the tide. No wonder the water never had a chance to warm up when it kept coming in and going back out twice every day.

Thinking about the cold water kept his mind off the octopus for a little way, but as he got closer to where he was heading he found himself feeling shaky and sick. What if the octopus hadn't been scared away by Bobbi? What if they were all waiting …

Cut it out! he told himself firmly. Octopus were no different from fish, or crabs, or anything else that lived in the ocean. Besides, he didn't have to go right into the semicircle of traps. He'd pick the closest one, cut a hole in the watertight liner, grab a couple of things from inside, and get out of there. It wouldn't take more than a minute.

He continued to swim, checking every few strokes to make sure he was following the right compass line. At last he spotted a marker buoy exactly where he'd expected it to be, followed by eleven more in a loose semi-circle. Taking a deep breath, he dove.

He could feel goosebumps racing across his shoulders as he sliced downward through the water. No octopus so far, he reassured himself, but he knew that didn't mean they wouldn't turn up. Still, at this rate he should be down and back up again pretty quickly. Nothing could happen in just a couple of minutes.

Something brushed against his leg! A jellyish octopus tenacle! He could see the rows of pale white suction cups all down its length.

His stomach turned. Before he could stop himself he

was vomiting and gasping for air. Instead, water filled his lungs. Frantically he pushed upwards.

Just as he, like Bobbi, was beginning to think he wasn't going to make it, he felt his head break the surface. Still vomiting and coughing he gasped in the fresh air and struggled to clear his lungs.

That was enough, he told himself when he finally stopped choking. Bobbi hadn't been able to do it twice, and neither could he. If he tried again and got sick again he'd drown for sure. And he was just about to start the long swim back when it occurred to him that the octopus tenacle had been yucky and had made him throw up, but it hadn't been threatening or vicious. In fact, the owner of the tenacle had seemed just as eager to part company as he had.

Then should he try once again to get that proof?

No! he told himself firmly, remembering those minutes of struggling for air when he'd started to vomit.

But he couldn't get sick again, he told himself, because there was nothing left to get sick with. Besides, he'd just remembered something — Jock's message to Dad. Jock had admitted that he didn't like octopus but he'd gone on to say that they were only dangerous when their eight arms were divided by four. Had he been trying to tell Dad that the spawning area was only dangerous when there were two legs — in other words, *humans* — around? Had he stumbled on plans for the proposed housebreaking scam — guessed that they were planning to use his prawn traps for hiding the stolen goods — and discovered that Devon had put those traps in the spawning ground this year? Jock wanted Dad to check it out, but he was afraid Dad might freak out at the sight of the spawning beds, so he was trying to tell Dad there was nothing to worry about — that octopus weren't scary.

Jock wouldn't have said that if it wasn't true, Lion told himself.

He took several deep breaths, waited for his heart to stop pounding, and dove back down. This time, within seconds he had reached one of the prawn traps — sitting as Devon had said, near a rock crevasse.

Half in and half out of the crevasse were two octopus!

The blanket of panic started once again to wrap itself around him. *Concentrate!* he told himself angrily, pushing the panic away. *Ignore the octopus. They aren't interested in you. Get that proof and get out of here.*

Turning his back he moved close to the trap, made a wide hole in the thick plastic liner with one sweeping slash of Bobbi's knife, grabbed the first two things he could feel and headed back up to the surface.

His first thought as his head broke through and fresh air filled his lungs was that now he could throw up if he wanted to! His second thought was curiosity over what he'd brought with him. He looked down. One hand held a camera in a leather case, the other held a gold wrist watch.

Then he remembered the liners — the thick shiny black plastic liners — exactly like that piece of black plastic Bobbi had found in C.J.'s closet! C.J. had worked out what was going on and where the stuff had been hidden! He had taken the piece of plastic liner as proof! And they'd found out. That's why they'd decided to make sure he couldn't tell his story to anyone!

He slipped the gold watch over one wrist and put the strap of the camera case around his neck. Then, steadying the camera against his body with one hand so the moving ocean water wouldn't pull it off, he made his way slowly back through the cold water to the end of the wharf.

Chapter 20

Bobbi was waiting when Lion reached the end of the wooden wharf. Her face was anxious. "Are you all right? Did you get sick?"

"Yes, to both questions," Lion told her grinning. "But I got the proof." He held up the watch and the camera.

Bobbi beamed at him. She took the things he was holding and set them on the wharf. "Thanks for going down, Lion," she told him quietly as he climbed out of the water. Then before he realized what she was intending, she wrapped both arms around his waist and hugged him. "I was worried," she admitted in a funny thick voice.

Frantically Lion pulled free. What if she tried to kiss him! "Come on, Bobbi. Don't be dumb! There was nothing to worry about. It was just a simple dive. I'm fine."

It was obvious from Bobbi's expression that she didn't believe him, but the danger was past. Instead of kissing him, she was peering at him closely. "Since when is green and exhausted the latest style in fine?" But her voice was back to normal.

"Forget green and exhausted," Lion returned. He glanced along the shore. The shadows were so thick and heavy they could no longer see Jock's house. "Now we'd better find C.J.", he said in a tight scared voice. "Because whoever planted that bug in C.J.'s room may have checked out the closet first and seen the piece of plastic liner. That may be how they knew he was on to them."

Bobbi shivered. She glanced out toward the fishing boat. "I'll go out first while you catch your breath and see where they've got him. Then we can work out a rescue plan."

Though he wasn't about to admit it, Lion was glad he didn't have to swim back out in that freezing water right away. Bobbi was right, he did feel kind of awful. He peeled off the wet suit and gave it to her.

Moments later Bobbi was letting herself down into the water.

It was much longer than Lion expected before she re-appeared, and when she did she was exhausted.

"What took you so long?" The growing worry he'd been feeling found release in anger.

"The tide," Bobbi replied breathlessly. "It's really coming in fast. Swimming against the undertow is awful."

"Never mind the tide, did you find C.J.?"

"Mmmm-hmmm — but he's either hurt, or drugged." Bobbi's voice was scared. "I banged as hard as I could on the porthole window right beside where he was lying to let him know we were coming to help, but he didn't even move."

For a moment after that there was silence. Then Bobbi continued in the same breathless rush, "If I could hardly swim back in against the undertow, he'll never be able to do it."

Needling at the back of Lion's mind all the time they'd been sitting at the end of the dock was why Devon hadn't done anything to chase them away. Suddenly he had the answer. Devon knew they wouldn't dare do anything till after dark — not when they knew he was watching — and by the time it was dark it would be too late. By then the tide would be full. That's why he'd made that crack about not going swimming — that the undertow was too dangerous. He wanted to plant the idea that they'd never be able to rescue C.J. and swim back against the undertow, so they wouldn't even attempt it. And then if they did go ahead and got drowned in the process, he could make the excuse that he'd tried to warn them.

He told Bobbi what he was thinking. "What are we gonna do?" he finished.

Bobbi was watching the water splashing against the supporting pylons of the wharf. It was already three times as high as it had been earlier. And as each huge wave crashed onto the shore the water rolled over and instantly reversed with a powerful suction motion. "That's what's so dangerous," Bobbi said pointing. "That undertow. That's why it took me so long to swim back from the boat."

"What are we gonna do?" Lion said again, struggling to keep his teeth from chattering. If C.J. was as cold as he was —

"I don't know," Bobbi admitted.

For the next few minutes they sat in gloomy silence. Then all at once Bobbi's face brightened. "The horses!" she exclaimed.

"Pardon?"

Instead of answering she got to her feet and started down the wharf, stopping and peering around each boat mooring pylon, and looking into every life jacket locker. At last she turned and started back to where Lion was waiting. Smiling broadly she held up what she had found — three lengths of water-buoyant ski rope.

Lion gave her a puzzled stare. "What's so great about those?"

Bobbi's grin widened. "We'll tie these three ropes together, and if they're long enough nobody will have to swim back in. We'll wrap C.J. in a life jacket, attach one end of the rope to him and to whoever goes out to get him, and then let one of the horses pull everybody in."

Chapter 21

As they made their way back along the deserted wharf toward where they had left the horses tethered, Bobbi explained what she had in mind.

Lion wasn't impressed. Maybe some horses might rise to the occasion and be heroes, but he wasn't so sure about his. If C.J. needed rescuing, Brie had better be ready to do it.

But he didn't say so. Instead, glancing at the pounding waves that seemed to be steadily growing in size and power, he said, "Aren't those waves going to terrify the horses?"

"Mmm-hmmm."

"Then what's the point in kidding ourselves that they'll be any help?"

"Just because they're scared it doesn't mean they'll refuse to co-operate."

"Speak for your own horse," Lion muttered under his breath.

Bobbi grinned. "Actually, one horse is all we need."

They'd reached the trees where the horses were waiting. At their approach Raj threw up his head and snorted impatiently.

"He's mad at having been tied up all this time," Lion muttered.

Ignoring him, Bobbi moved past Raj and untied Brie. Then, still holding the ski ropes, she started back down the beach, reassuring the mare gently with each step. She took her down the rocky shoreline to the edge of the water, then when her feet were wet let her stop. "I'll give her a chance to get used to it," she said.

A wave broke around Brie's feet. It was fairly small and gentle. Brie picked up her front hoofs one after the other, but made no other protest.

However the next wave must have been a seventh one. Not only did it hit the beach with a crashing roar, it swirled around Brie's feet with startling force and splashed up cold against her underbelly.

Brie reared back so unexpectedly that the reins slipped through Bobbi's grasp. Before Bobbi could grab them again, Brie was racing back toward the shore, up the beach, toward the road, and seconds later had disappeared into the foliage on the other side.

"Heaven knows when she'll finally stop," Bobbi moaned. "We haven't time to waste trying to find her."

"So, now what?"

"We'll have to use Raj." Bobbi headed back toward the trees.

"Come on, Bobbi!" Lion protested, moving after her. "That's an even bigger waste of time than chasing after Brie. If your horse won't go in the waves there's no way that one of mine will."

Bobbi paid no attention. She untied Raj.

He looked even more unenthusiastic than before. It was all Lion could do not to laugh.

Wrapping the reins firmly around her hand so Raj couldn't do an imitation of Brie's disappearing act, Bobbi turned her attention to the girth on Raj's saddle. "I should have known better than to expect a horse to go into those waves just being led," she said matter-of-factly, still concentrating on the girth. "Since they can't see any reason for going in, of course they're not going to do it. But if someone is on their back it's different. They're trained to do all sorts of things they don't particularly want to do when their rider tells them."

Lion's eyes rolled briefly skyward. "Well, it's your life, I guess. But are you sure you shouldn't reconsider? This is Raj you're planning to ride, remember?"

"Not me," Bobbi returned innocently. "Here. I'll give you a leg up."

"Me? No way!" Lion protested, backing away.

Bobbi's smile faded. "You've got to, Lion, because it's the only way we can help C.J. Raj will do it for you because he knows you."

"That's the whole reason he won't do it! Because he hates me."

"Don't be dumb." Bobbi continued to hold out the reins. "Remember how he helped you up at Wells? All you've got to do is let him know you're really depending on him."

"Great. And just how do I do that?"

"Talk to him. Take him slowly. Let him see and feel the water. If he hesitates, reassure him. Then, just as you did jumping that log in the pasture, 'think' him into doing what you want him to do."

"Think him out into the water?"

"Not too far. Just about half way."

Lion gave his sister a wary glance. "Why?"

"So I can tie one end of these ski ropes onto your saddle, and the other end onto C.J.'s life jacket."

"How d'you know he's wearing a life jacket?"

"He isn't. But there's sure to be one somewhere on that fishing boat, and I'll put it on him." As she'd been talking, she'd tied the three ropes together. "Then when I start back with C.J., even if he is hurt or only half conscious it'll be all right. We won't have to swim. All we'll have to do is float on top of the surface while you and Raj pull us back through the undertow."

Since it seemed to be their only chance, Lion

reluctantly agreed, but he knew before he started that it wouldn't work. It showed on his face.

"Come on, Lion! You've got to think positively! Just like in the pasture. Nobody would ever get a horse over a tough jump if he thought ahead of time that they'd never make it! Horses sense what you're thinking! You've got to picture doing it!"

But as Lion settled into the saddle Raj turned his head and gave him a cold, unco-operative glare.

"Don't complain to me," Lion told the big horse. "Complain to her." He nodded at his sister. "I don't want to do this any more than you do — "

"Please, Lion!" Bobbi begged. "Don't tell him that. Convince him it's the right thing! Think him into it!"

Reluctantly Lion revised his thinking. He moved Raj toward the waves.

Raj watched each one suspiciously, and hesitated each time one broke, but when Lion continued to urge him, Raj continued to move forward.

Bobbi, still in the wet suit, walked quietly beside them. "Move into the water till it's over his hooves then stop," she said in a calm, unhurried voice. "Meanwhile I'll start swimming out to the boat. By the time I'm about two thirds of the way you'll feel the slack starting to come out of the rope. That will be your signal to start moving Raj deeper into the water." She grinned. "Let's hope you don't have to move him in too deep — like till it's over his head."

"Can horses swim?" Lion asked anxiously.

"*Can* but not necessarily *will*," Bobbi replied, struggling to hide her grin. "I'm not sure how Raj feels about cold water."

Lion hoped she was kidding but he wasn't sure. "You think the ropes might not be long enough to stretch the whole way unless we go in pretty deep?" He wished his sister hadn't raised that possibility.

Bobbi took pity on him. "Actually, I'm pretty sure they will be long enough. We've got three lengths of rope tied together — each one about 150 feet. That should reach to the boat without Raj having to go in very far at all." She glanced thoughtfully down at the waves. "At least it should if we go before the tide gets any higher."

"Then stop talking and go!" Lion urged.

As they'd been talking Bobbi had been readjusting the wet suit. Now she tied her end of the ski rope around her waist, knotted it securely so she couldn't possibly lose it, and started to move off.

"Bobbi wait!" Lion called in a hoarse whisper. He glanced nervously around at the shadowy darkness. "What if Devon and his friends decide they aren't going to just sit back and watch? What if they decide to make sure we can't get out there to help C.J.?"

"Improvise. Who knows, Raj may find he likes swimming."

Lion had the distinct impression that his sister was laughing as she moved away. He watched till he could no longer see her against the waves, then he had no choice but to move into phase two. He gave Raj a nervous pat, then carefully, one step at a time, he began inching him deeper into the water.

Chapter 22

Bobbi had said he had to use positive thinking and mental telepathy if he expected Raj to keep going. It obviously hadn't occurred to her that he might not be thinking all that positively himself. However, it was too late to worry about that now. If she was right and mental telepathy did work on horses, then he'd better not admit even to himself how scared he was, or Raj would have them back in that nice quiet clump of trees in about two seconds. Carefully following instructions, he "pictured" them moving slowly out deeper.

To his amazement, Raj obeyed. Not exactly with enthusiasm, but he didn't plant his forefeet and refuse.

Fortunately, at this particular point the ocean floor dropped very gradually. They managed ten metres with the water still only knee deep. But Lion knew trouble was coming, for already the waves were splashing up wet and cold under Raj's stomach. When they really started to hit him —

Better to leave that thought unfinished too, he decided, remembering about mental telepathy.

He'd already checked the triple ski rope at least a dozen times, but he checked it again. It was still floating in slack relaxed circles on the water. Maybe they were going to luck out and the rope was going to be long enough after all.

He continued to inch Rajah deeper.

The rope in front of him began to tighten. Most of the slack was gone and the water was inching up to the big horse's shoulders. How much farther would they have to go? What if Bobbi was wrong about the rope being long enough?

Just as he was sure Raj was going to have to swim whether he liked it or not, Lion felt the signal he'd been praying for. Three quick tugs, a pause, then three more tugs. Bobbi said she'd send that signal when she reached the fishing boat and again when she had C.J. in a life jacket and ready for Lion to start hand-over-handing back on the rope to pull them in.

Impatiently Lion waited.

Suddenly a new worry surfaced. *Were Devon and the van driver watching? Did they guess what was up?* Mental telepathy, Lion reminded himself sternly! If Raj sensed what he was thinking and realized how scared he was …!

But this time his fears refused to be pushed away. He could feel the goosebumps running across his shoulders. Again his teeth began chattering, and this time it wasn't because of the cold.

Hurry up, Bobbi!

At last through his mounting panic he felt the second signal come along the ski rope. Bobbi had C.J. ready! Tightening his reins to keep Raj motionless, and watching the rope to make sure he didn't give a sudden jerk which might dislodge his passengers at the other end, he began pulling the rope back in.

It was harder work than he'd expected. But Bobbi and C.J. must be being pulled shoreward for the rope was steadily coming in.

Suddenly the muscles along Raj's back tightened. His head came up. He swung it backward.

Quickly Lion looked back to see what Raj had heard, and his throat closed in panic. He now knew the answer to the question he'd asked himself earlier about what Devon and the van driver were doing. They were standing on the beach directly behind him. In the moonlight reflecting off the water he could see them clearly.

He had to warn Bobbi. But how? If he stopped pulling on the rope as a signal that there was trouble, C.J. might be submerged by the waves and the suction of the undertow. If he didn't stop pulling, Bobbi would assume everything was okay. She'd have no warning that Devon and the van driver were waiting for them as soon as they came close enough.

Desperately, Lion looked back toward the stretch of highway that edged the area of ocean directly behind where he and Raj were standing. All sorts of cars were driving by — he could see their lights. If only there was some way he could signal one of them. Between pulls on the rope he waved one hand high over his head. But though lots of drivers slowed to look at the view, nobody noticed his waving, or if they did they paid no attention.

No! Somebody *had* stopped! A man was getting out of his car. He was moving directly toward them!

Lion's heart gave a leap, for it was Mr. Rutner!

He must have got the message Bobbi left on his answering machine. They were going to be okay after all!

"Over here, Mr. Rutner!" he called urgently. "Over here! C.J.'s hurt and my sister's bringing him in! We need you to help us!"

For a second, the approaching figure seemed startled at his words. Mr. Rutner broke stride and almost stopped. Then he started walking again, calling in an amused voice, "Of course I'll help you. That's why I've come. Mr. Fix-it on the way!"

All at once Lion was uneasy. What did he mean, that's why he'd come? How could he have known they were on the beach? Bobbi hadn't mentioned that in her message. All she'd said was that she and Lion were looking for C.J.

and were wondering if Mr. Rutner had seen him or knew where he might be. It was all very well to be a Mr. Fix-it but —

Mr. Fix-It!

Lion's uneasiness changed to cold fear. Frantically he started pulling harder on the rope, trying to get Bobbi and C.J. close enough to warn them. For Mr. Rutner had called himself Mr. Fix-it once before, he remembered — on the morning he'd been doing all those odd jobs for Mrs. Hamilton. One of the jobs had been in C.J.'s bedroom. He'd done it while C.J. was out. But when Lion mentioned it later, C.J. hadn't seemed to know anything about it.

What if the job Rutner had been doing wasn't fixing a light socket as he'd claimed, but putting that bug behind C.J.'s dresser — the bug Bobbi discovered the very next day! What if while he'd been looking for a place to put the bug he'd seen the piece of torn plastic liner that C.J. had hidden in his closet?

And now Lion remembered something else. That first day Rutner said they'd been smart to choose the ferry they did from Horseshoe Bay — that there'd have been a huge wait if they'd come any later. How could he have known which ferry they'd taken unless the van driver had told him!

The cold fear turned to panic. Rutner hadn't come down to the beach because of Bobbi's message at all. *He must have received another one from Devon or the van driver! He was in this with them!*

Something else was pulling at the back of Lion's mind as well — something someone had said about Rutner — but right now there were too many more important things to worry about.

He peered even more anxiously into the distance, looking for any sign of his sister and C.J. through the choppy waves. "Bobbi?" he called as loudly as he dared. He tugged harder on the rope. He had to warn them. Somehow they had to find a different place for C.J. to come ashore. "Bobbi?" he called again.

Still no answer.

Just as he was sure something must have happened, he saw something moving in the shadowy greyness. Seconds later Bobbi and C.J. had reached him and Raj.

"We've got to find somewhere else to go in to shore," Lion warned in a quick frightened whisper, knowing how easily voices travelled over water. "Devon and the van driver are on the beach, waiting for us, and Rutner's just joined them."

Bobbi gasped in shock. "You mean he's in it too?" A moment earlier she'd been smiling, but now her eyes darkened with fear.

At the mention of Rutner's name, C.J.'s head came up. Though he was close to exhaustion he said faintly, "Why would — he need to — get involved in a — money grab?"

At C.J.'s words the thought that had been eluding Lion swam to the surface. He turned to C.J. "When we were talking that first evening you said Rutner was loaded — that he owned half the shares in the town's biggest industry. What is the town's biggest industry?" Even before C.J. answered Lion knew what the answer would be. Pulp and paper.

Everything fell into place. That's why Devon and Rutner and the van driver had tried to stop Dad from talking to Jock — because Dad had those report figures! That's why C.J. had been set up as fall-guy in the housebreaking scam — to discredit his mom, so she'd no longer be listened to about banning the pulp mill effluent. That might even be why Rutner was buttering up Mrs. Hamilton — figuring if the disgrace of having a housebreaking son wasn't enough to discredit her, he could personally persuade her to stop her anti-pulp-mill effluent campaign.

If only he'd worked it all out sooner. Now it was too late.

Again he glanced at the shore. The three men had formed themselves into a solid line waiting for them.

"Think," Lion said in a low urgent voice, turning to C.J. "Where else can we go ashore?"

"There isn't — any place." C.J.'s voice was so faint Lion could hardly hear. "Every place — else — too rocky. — waves would smash us to bits." He sounded frightened now too.

But Bobbi had recovered. "Then Lion's got to get down and you've got to get up on Raj," she told C.J. matter-of-factly. Already she was untying the life jacket from around him. "Do you think you can stay on?"

C.J. nodded.

Lion was sure he couldn't. He looked ill and exhausted. His whole body was shivering and his face was colourless. But Bobbi was waiting for Lion to dismount, so he swung unenthusiastically down into the cold chest-high water, then helped Bobbi push C.J up into the saddle in his place.

As they worked, Bobbi explained her plan. When Lion and C.J. had run out of objections and questions, she asked C.J., "Ready?"

He nodded.

Bobbi glanced over at Lion. As arranged they moved up one on either side of Raj, each with a hand on C.J. as if he was too weak to stay on unassisted. Then in a group they started toward the men on the shore. They were a sorry sight — heads down, shoulders slumped, eyes defeated, steps slow.

They were close enough now to see the smug grins

on the faces of the three men waiting for them. For a moment Lion wondered just what was planned for them if this scheme of Bobbi's failed, but he decided he'd just as soon not know.

"Get ready," Bobbi warned under her breath.

They were now only a couple of dozen paces from the waiting men. Bobbi waited while they took another five paces, then said quietly, "Now!" As she spoke she stepped clear of Raj.

Following the orders Bobbi had given them earlier, Lion also stepped clear of Raj, and C.J. dug his heels hard into the big horse's flanks.

The plan was that C.J. would gallop full speed right through the men, for as Bobbi had explained few people will try to stop a galloping horse. "It's why mounted policemen are so great for mob control," she'd added.

But she hadn't bargained on C.J.'s exhaustion. What should have been a sharp dig was little more than a nudge. Raj looked back disapprovingly, as if to say that he was exhausted too, and continued at the same lazy pace.

The men were almost on them.

Bobbi didn't wait. Grabbing the end of one of the ski ropes she gave Raj a sharp slap across his flank.

He was so surprised fatigue was forgotten. He took off at full gallop.

As Bobbi had prophesied, all three men jumped back and dodged out of the way. By the time they'd recovered, C.J. and Raj were fifty yards up the shore.

Lion meanwhile, running as fast as he could, had disappeared into the shadows down the beach, well to the left of where the men were standing. As soon as he was safely out of sight, he stopped and looked back. With alarm he realized that C.J. was only barely managing to stay on Raj's back. In about two more minutes he'd be off for sure. He'd never make it safely back to the house. Lion had to do something to help, but what?

He turned the other way to check on Bobbi, who according to plan had raced for the shadows to the right of the men while Lion had gone to the left. Bobbi was in even more trouble than C.J.! Why hadn't he realized how exhausted she'd be after that long swim? He should have insisted they stay together so he could help her! He should have realized she would never be able to outrun those men — particularly not when she was wearing a bulky wet suit that was two sizes too big!

Even as he watched, Devon caught her.

Leaving his cover Lion raced back to help. But before he'd taken more than half a dozen steps, he stopped again, for Devon had let Bobbi go. Now what was he planning?

Instead of planning some new form of attack, Devon was moving back beside the other two men.

At last Lion understood. All three were staring toward the highway where another car had stopped. This time it was a familiar looking one. Three people had jumped out and were running toward them — Dad, Mrs. Hamilton and Martin Carswell.

Dad had got Bobbi's message!

Chapter 23

Just before noon next morning, Dad, Bobbi, Lion and C.J. all presented themselves at the reception desk in the hospital. To Lion's relief the nurse on duty was not the same one who'd been there the other time. This time when Dad asked permission to visit Mr. McPherson there was no objection.

Jock was still pale and ill looking but he beamed when he saw them. Then his glance settled on Bobbi and Lion. "Thank you," he told them simply. "I've heard what you did."

Lion could feel the blood creeping into his cheeks. He felt like an idiot — until he realized his two-years-older-and-much-more-sophisticated-sister was blushing too. Then he felt better.

"Any chance you might stay around for a while till they let me out of here, so we can go fishing?" Jock asked, turning to Dad.

"Wish I could," Dad replied, shaking his head.

"Don't you ever take a break from that business of yours?"

"Actually, this time it isn't business. I've got some wedding plans to help arrange. The bride is Virginia Hamilton."

Lion's world crashed! Dad was getting remarried after all! He wasn't even going to try to get back with Mom. He was going to marry Mrs. Hamilton! They'd end up moving here, because now that C.J. had been cleared there'd be no reason why his mom wouldn't be elected permanent principal, and it would be her Middle School that Lion would be enrolled in come September!

"Of course," Jock's voice broke into Lion's panic. "She's the woman who's done such a great job of alerting people to the possible harmful effects of pulp mill effluent on marine life."

Dad nodded. "The groom is Martin Carswell."

With a rush Lion came back to life. He looked up to find Dad watching him, his eyes alive with amusement.

Dad had been conning him! Dad had guessed what he'd been thinking and deliberately led him along! But he was so relieved to discover that he wasn't getting a Middle School principal for a mother after all that he just grinned.

"Yeah, it's great," C.J. was saying shyly from across the room. "Will you come up for the wedding?"

Lion was just about to explain that they probably wouldn't be able to come for the wedding because Dad would be too busy working, when he realized that C.J. hadn't been talking to him at all. He was talking to Bobbi — gazing at her with a dumb moony expression.

She didn't seem to think it was dumb or moony at all! "Of course," she said, smiling up at him.

Lion couldn't believe it! Not even an "I'll have to see" or "I'll have to ask Dad". Just a sickly "Of course!" What was wrong with everybody? First Dad, and now Bobbi!

Well, maybe everybody else was only interested in love, but there were some questions he wanted answered. Leaving Bobbi and C.J to moon at each other, he turned back to Dad.

"Using the traps as the hiding place for the loot was just extra insurance, right? To discredit Jock in case they didn't succeed in stopping him from finishing that report?"

Dad nodded. "It made it easy when Devon was Jock's

partner. They probably planned to leave just enough evidence behind after they moved the stuff out so that Jock would be arrested."

"And C.J. was set up as fall-guy to discredit his mom."

Again Dad nodded.

"It was just their bad luck that I came up earlier than usual this year," Jock said in an amused tone from his bed. "I fooled them."

"Don't boast," Dad told him wryly. "You nearly got killed for your pains." He looked at his watch. "Now, unfortunately, we've got to go. I've got business waiting back in Vancouver." He got to his feet.

They were in the car heading back down the highway when Dad said quietly, "You two did a great job." He was watching Lion in the rearview mirror and a soft light came into his eyes. "Particularly for going down to get the proof we had to have in the middle of those octopus beds. I know how you feel about octopus."

Lion stared in delight. It wasn't often Dad actually sounded impressed. "Bobbi went down first, and she was just as scared."

"I know. I'm proud of both of you."

Lion was still basking in the unusual approval when Dad added, "I hesitate to say so, but I hate to think what might have happened if you two hadn't been along on this trip."

"Does that mean we can help on all your cases?" Lion asked eagerly.

"No, it does not," Dad returned. "You know the rules. If you come along on a case you are to stay right out of my business."

"But what if you need us!" Lion protested.

For a minute Dad's eyes in the rearview mirror continued to frown, then a quizzical smile pulled at the corners. "Well, that's different," he admitted.

Lion sat back, beaming. So who cared if the kids did sometimes get on his back. Maybe it wasn't so bad being a famous lawyer's kid after all.

Joan Weir is an accomplished writer for young readers with numerous books to her credit, including *The Witcher*, which is the first book in the Lion and Bobbi Mysteries series. Other books include *Sixteen is Spelled O-U-C-H* (Stoddart, 1996) and *Mystery at Lighthouse Rock* (Stoddart, 1991). She is a creative writing instructor at the University College of the Cariboo. Joan Weir lives — and rides her horse, Raj, who is the model for Lion's horse — in Kamloops, British Columbia.

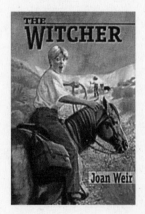

THE WITCHER *by Joan Weir*
witcher\'wich-er*n*: one who uses a divining rod to seek the location of water or minerals underground.

The first Lion and Bobbi Mystery is a funny, fast-paced and scary story that will enthrall mystery buffs to the very last word.

"Take an intriguing title, add a mystery, include a dash of danger, a bantering family and a hate-love relationship with a horse, and you've got the ingredients for a book that will please a wide-ranging audience. *The Witcher* will hook young readers."

— *Quill & Quire*

More Books for Young Readers from Polestar:

DogStar   *by Beverley Wood and Chris Wood*
1-896095-37-2 • $8.95 in Canada • $6.95 in USA
This time-travel adventure story introduces 12-year-old Jeff and Bull Terrier Patsy Ann.

Dreamcatcher   *by Meredy Maynard*
1-896095-01-1 • $9.95 in Canada • $7.50 in USA
A 13-year-old boy comes to terms with the death of his father.

Great Canadian Scientists   *by Barry Shell*
1-896095-36-4 • $18.95 in Canada • $14.95 in USA
In-depth profiles of 19 of Canada's most interesting scientists. With activities, photos and illustrations, a detailed glossary and brief bios of 120 other women and men of science.

One In A Million   *by Nicholas Read*
1-896095-22-4 • $8.95 in Canada • $6.95 in USA
The story of a dog named Joey, from his abandonment at a shelter through his unhappy days as a street waif to his joyous adoption.

Starshine!   *by Ellen Schwartz*
0-919591-24-8 • $8.95 in Canada • $5.95 in USA
Starshine Bliss Shapiro tackles life's problems with the help of her hobby — spiders! Also in the series: Starshine at Camp Crescent Moon and Starshine on TV.

Witch's Fang   *by Heather Kellerhals-Stewart*
0-919591-88-4 • $9.95 in Canada • $7.95 in USA
Three teens risk their lives in this mountain-climbing adventure.

The Witcher   *by Joan Weir*
1-896095-98-4 • $8.95 in Canada • $6.95 in USA
The first Lion and Bobbi Mystery. "The Witcher will hook young readers." — Quill & Quire

Polestar books are available at your favourite bookstore.
For a complete list of our titles, contact us at:
POLESTAR BOOK PUBLISHERS
P.O. Box 5238, Station B
Victoria, British Columbia
Canada V8R 6N4
http://mypage.direct.ca/p/polestar/